A Candlelight Ecstasy Romance®

"DO YOU ALWAYS GET YOUR WAY?"

She tilted her head to better examine his strong profile.

"Always," he admitted. He stopped for a traffic light and turned to meet her examining gaze. "Let that be lesson number one to you, Miss Hannah Blake." Yale's smokey eyes rested on her curved lips and she was aghast over how they involuntarily softened and parted slightly.

"I'm not likely to be concerned over any such lesson," she returned, trying to hide her sudden breathlessness.

"Is that a challenge, Ms. Blake?" he asked silkily. "Lesson number two that you'll have to learn is that I never refuse a challenge."

A CANDLELIGHT ECSTASY ROMANCE ®

146 PASSION AND ILLUSION, *Bonnie Drake*
147 LOVE'S UNVEILING, *Samantha Scott*
148 MOONLIGHT RAPTURE, *Prudence Martin*
149 WITH EVERY LOVING TOUCH, *Nell Kincaid*
150 ONE OF A KIND, *Jo Calloway*
151 PRIME TIME, *Rachel Ryan*
152 AUTUMN FIRES, *Jackie Black*
153 ON WINGS OF MAGIC, *Kay Hooper*
154 A SEASON FOR LOVE, *Heather Graham*
155 LOVING ADVERSARIES, *Eileen Bryan*
156 KISS THE TEARS AWAY, *Anna Hudson*
157 WILDFIRE, *Cathie Linz*
158 DESIRE AND CONQUER, *Diane Dunaway*
159 A FLIGHT OF SPLENDOR, *Joellyn Carroll*
160 FOOL'S PARADISE, *Linda Vail*
161 A DANGEROUS HAVEN, *Shirley Hart*
162 VIDEO VIXEN, *Elaine Raco Chase*
163 BRIAN'S CAPTIVE, *Alexis Hill Jordan*
164 ILLUSIVE LOVER, *Jo Calloway*
165 A PASSIONATE VENTURE, *Julia Howard*
166 NO PROMISE GIVEN, *Donna Kimel Vitek*
167 BENEATH THE WILLOW TREE, *Emma Bennett*
168 CHAMPAGNE FLIGHT, *Prudence Martin*
169 INTERLUDE OF LOVE, *Beverly Sommers*
170 PROMISES IN THE NIGHT, *Jackie Black*
171 HOLD LOVE TIGHTLY, *Megan Lane*
172 ENDURING LOVE, *Tate McKenna*
173 RESTLESS WIND, *Margaret Dobson*
174 TEMPESTUOUS CHALLENGE, *Eleanor Woods*
175 TENDER TORMENT, *Harper McBride*
176 PASSIONATE DECEIVER, *Barbara Andrews*
177 QUIET WALKS THE TIGER, *Heather Graham*
178 A SUMMER'S EMBRACE, *Cathie Linz*
179 DESERT SPLENDOR, *Samantha Hughes*
180 LOST WITHOUT LOVE, *Elizabeth Raffel*
181 A TEMPTING STRANGER, *Lori Copeland*
182 DELICATE BALANCE, *Emily Elliott*
183 A NIGHT TO REMEMBER, *Shirley Hart*
184 DARK SURRENDER, *Diana Blayne*
185 TURN BACK THE DAWN, *Nell Kincaid*

NO OTHER LOVE

Alyssa Morgan

A CANDLELIGHT ECSTASY ROMANCE ®

Published by
Dell Publishing Co., Inc.
1 Dag Hammarskjold Plaza
New York, New York 10017

ISBN: 0–440–16328–5

Printed in the United States of America
First printing—November 1983

To Our Readers:

We have been delighted with your enthusiastic response to Candlelight Ecstasy Romances®, and we thank you for the interest you have shown in this exciting series.

In the upcoming months we will continue to present the distinctive sensuous love stories you have come to expect only from Ecstasy. We look forward to bringing you many more books from your favorite authors and also the very finest work from new authors of contemporary romantic fiction.

As always, we are striving to present the unique, absorbing love stories that you enjoy most—books that are more than ordinary romance.

Your suggestions and comments are always welcome. Please write to us at the address below.

Sincerely,

The Editors
Candlelight Romances
1 Dag Hammarskjold Plaza
New York, New York 10017

CHAPTER ONE

Hannah tossed the weed into the basket and sat back on her haunches to survey the cleaned rose bed with a feeling of satisfaction. She'd made it her project during her two weeks of enforced idleness and it was ready now for the mulching.

"Woof?" The black labrador's bark was a challenging question as he placed the stick at her feet.

A wide grin parted her generous mouth. "Okay, Boston, you've been admirably patient. Now it's play time." She picked up the stick and sent it in a high arc. It gave a satisfying splash on landing in the nearby lake. Boston's yelp held pure joy as he bounded after it.

"Enough!" She laughed after a dozen throws. "You've succeeded in getting me properly wet. Besides, you look absolutely foolish with your tongue hanging to the ground." She gave the dripping dog a hug and turned back to the house, giving a passing rueful look at her once spotless yellow halter and abbreviated shorts, now both wet and dirt-smudged. At least her labors had revived her tan, she noticed, eyeing the golden glow to her long limbs.

She kicked off her muddy sneakers at the back entrance and gave the dog a reproving look as he tried to inch through the half-open screen door. "You better not dare, Boston!" she scolded. "Letta will have your head if you track those muddy feet on her clean floors."

The dog gave a resigned sigh before trotting to a sunny spot to sink on the grass. He stared at her reproachfully, his head resting on his paws.

"It won't work," she cried, her stern frown at variance with the laughter lurking in her amber eyes. Only then did she notice her father's Mercedes was in the garage, and she hurried inside.

She paused in the kitchen to sneak a stalk of celery Letta was preparing for a salad. She grinned on catching the threatening look before the maid chuckled, white teeth flashing against ebony skin.

"Better save your appetite, Miss Hannah. I made your favorite chocolate cake. Have to put some meat on you while we have you here!" Dark brown eyes gazed with affection at the tall slender girl. "Not that you don't have all the right curves—you just need a little more accent!" Ample shoulders moved in laughter at the pretended look of outrage Hannah tossed her.

"I'll have you know that last night I was told I was model material," she said as she swayed around the table in an undulating sensual glide in imitation of a high-fashion mannequin. She stopped by Letta and gave her a hug. What would they have done without the tender ministrations of this white-haired woman over the years?

She sneaked another stalk of celery and sailed out of the room to the library-study where she knew her father always relaxed.

"Dad," she sang out on seeing him. "I want to be properly thanked. Your rose bed is all weeded and ready for your inspection." She went to the tall man where he stood by the book-lined shelves and raised her face for his kiss.

He responded before shaking his head, his expression one of resignation as he took in her disheveled appearance. "Don't tell me. You and Boston were in the lake again. I don't believe either one of you will ever grow up."

"Do you want me to?" she challenged as she chomped down on the celery.

They were remarkably alike, tall with thick, tawny blond hair and amber eyes. She always related him to a lion, not realizing that as his cub, it made her a young, sleek lioness.

"What brings you home so early?" she asked. She leaned back on the desk with one hand, stretching to ease the muscles cramped from stooping over the rose bed. The gold ankle bracelet twinkled as her long, tanned legs extended in golden enticement. She was quite unaware of the feline grace of her action. At twenty-seven, her body had reached its full potential.

"Yale needed a reference book I happen to have," he answered, nodding to the other side of the room, and only then was Hannah aware that someone else was in the room.

Danger. The red-flagged warning leaped to mind as her eyes widened on seeing the tall dark man. Black, sleek, bottled danger with black hair fashionably styled and heavy brows over rugged features. Even his eyes were a dark smoky gray. He was wearing a midnight blue silk knit shirt with gray slacks, a matching shade to his disturbing eyes.

"Yale Upton, my daughter, Hannah," her father said in introduction.

He closed the book he was holding, keeping a finger in place as a marker and came to her, moving on gliding silent feet. Long fingers closed firmly around her reluctantly offered hand.

"My pleasure," he murmured conventionally, the velvet purr of his voice holding amusement.

"I'm lucky to have her home for two weeks," her father explained. "She's had the misfortune to get a nasty case of the flu and I insisted she take time off to recuperate fully."

Smoky eyes swept over her high firm breasts, the narrow waist, and flat abdomen, the curve of her womanly hips, and down the long expanse of her shapely legs, lingering slightly at the fine gold chain circling one ankle. It was an itemized evaluation.

"I would say she looks quite . . . healthy now," he said smoothly, his gaze once more investigating her eyes.

She deliberately widened them in an affected innocence that denied that she was aware of his inventory. So he was going to play that game, was he?

"Yes, I'm afraid so," her father agreed, pulling another book from the shelf. "She's making noises about going back to work, which means we'll lose her." He gave her a worried look over his shoulder. "I just hope you don't get too involved with the social scene again, my dear. You play too hard and as a result had no resistance to that bug when it hit you."

Hannah gave him a bland smile. They'd happened to meet at three parties in two weeks and he was now certain that was her daily—or nightly—fare. She hadn't tried to disillusion him that two had been business affairs, as they had been for him.

"I'm certain Miss Blake has many . . . attributes . . . that guarantee a plethora of escorts." His smile was as politely bland as hers had been. His eyes began to look over her again, as if to reaffirm the data already assimilated, only this time there was a subtle difference that caused Hannah to suck in her breath.

A quick glance saw her father intent on searching for a particular volume on the shelves, and her gaze slid back to the man to find he had already reached her slender bare feet with their delicate arch and was beginning a slow, lingering return, his eyes smoking over the vital areas.

Enough was enough! she seethed, knowing there was nothing she could say with her father standing behind her. Her white teeth bared as she prepared to bite down on the celery to give vent to her frustration when a retaliatory idea hit her. Two could play the same game!

He was standing a bare three feet from her, so that she was aware of his faint musky odor. Her lips pursed in a provocative curve as she deliberately duplicated his examination.

He was in his mid-thirties, she guessed. Character lines had already formed, grooving his cheeks and fanning creases from the corner of his eyes. It was a strong face, showing assurance and control. His lips were firm but at this moment of relaxation she sensed the sensuality that underlined the sexual play he was indulging in. She could almost feel the impact they would have on her mouth.

She hurried on over his bronzed throat and her eyes were captured by the crisp, dark curl of hair exposed at the V formed by the open neck of his two-buttoned shirt. He had a wide chest, necessary to carry the broad sweep of his shoulders, tapering to his narrow waist and hips and long, muscular legs.

Remembering the reason for her blatant scrutiny, she, too, let her gaze linger on its return trip. The snug trousers hinted at his obvious virility. By the time she reached his chest, she was all too conscious of the increase in her pulse rate. The silk knit shirt clung to him as a second skin and when she looked into his eyes, she was jolted by the smoldering passion burning there.

Then he pulled his eyes from hers to stare with a strange intensity at her mouth. Only then did she realize that she'd been so intent on her examination that the stalk of celery was still poised at her mouth. It rested against her teeth and she had been unconsciously rubbing it along the succulent curve of her lower lip.

Slowly, with a deliberate sensual relish, she parted her teeth and clamped down on the crisp vegetable. His eyes swept up to meet her mocking ones and she was immediately enveloped in a swirling, smoky fire.

Her father's voice dragged her back from an unchartered distance. "You'd better change, Hannah," he said. "I've invited Yale to have lunch with us, and I'm sure you'll want to eradicate this first impression you've made."

God, had her father observed their private duel after all? She blinked in an effort to clear her mind and realized with a rush of relief that he was referring to the damp, revealing clothes she wore.

Their attention was diverted on hearing high heels clicking on the parquet floors in the hall. A breathtakingly lovely girl paused in the doorway before she came in to kiss her father.

"Have a good morning in art class, love?" he asked with indulgent interest.

"Oh, yes, Dad," she sighed, her blue eyes bright with stars. "Stan . . . Mr. Bryant said I had great potential!"

"He better," Hannah said dryly. "His outrageous fee should guarantee nothing less than a new generation of Picassos!" Debbie had come home a month before, sighing eloquently over the art teacher her *very dearest* friend was going to. Nothing would do but that she, too, took lessons. After seeing the effete Mr. Bryant, with his soulful brown eyes and long curly hair, she assured their father that there was nothing to worry about in this, the latest of her young seventeen-year-old sister's bouts with puppy love.

Debbie's mouth pursed. "You never liked him!" she protested. "You have no artistic soul and can never understand . . ."

"Spare me the details!" Hannah drawled. "I know I'm a hard-hearted career woman, emotionally barren, and . . . what was that latest colorful description you gave me? Ah, yes, a frustrated spinster bypassed by eligible men. Really, darling, you shouldn't take to heart those romantic stories you read!" Her younger sister had no knowledge of the number of men constantly phoning her.

Her lips twitched on seeing the tears hanging on her sister's lashes. When Debbie finally realized her potential as an actress, *then* she'd give her career her wholehearted support!

"You're a beast, you know," Debbie cried. Her blue eyes then grew round on seeing the dark man standing in the shadow of a bookcase.

Her father placed an arm around his youngest and made the introductions. "Debbie, meet our guest, Yale Upton." A dainty hand disappeared in the large tanned one.

"Debbie is such a childish name, don't you think?" she said with breathless eagerness, her hand fluttering to her hair, carrying attention to its lovely blond curls. "Deborah is much more mature."

Hannah rolled her eyes to the ceiling and groaned inwardly. Exit Stan Bryant, art teacher *extraordinaire,* and enter Yale Upton, dangerous hunter.

"And a very suitable name for a very charming young lady," he murmured as he smiled into the wide blue eyes regarding him with happy fascination.

Hannah watched with a detached cynicism as Yale

switched into a new character. She could almost believe the aggressive predator had been a figment of her imagination if lingering vibrations weren't still running along her nerves.

She noticed with resignation how Debbie opened like a rose to the sunshine of his attention as he listened with practiced interest while she described the painting that had indicated "great potential."

When death had taken their beloved mother two years ago, Hannah had to fight her inclination to become overly protective of her young sister. Her father, burying his grief in his successful law practice, was apt to give in to her every whim. She'd been indulgent with Debbie's harmless adulations over the opposite sex, naming them correctly as part of the process of growing up. But now, seeing the tall man listening with indolent attention to her prattle, she was conscious that her little sister was using all her feminine wiles.

But Yale Upton was way out of the league Debbie was used to playing in. He was arrogant, devastatingly assured, and too experienced. He definitely wasn't the man for a young woman to practice on. Even she knew it would be wise to back away from further contact with him. Any entanglement with him would lead only to heartache for her young sister.

Not that she need worry that a masculine sophisticate like Yale would consider one as inexperienced as her sister, but from past performances she knew Debbie all too well. Somehow she'd contrive further encounters, and she could imagine his annoyance on finding her crop up unexpectedly to include herself in whatever he was doing. She only hoped in his exasperation he didn't slap her down too hard.

Debbie, she knew, could at times be a royal pain in the neck, but her aura of sweet innocence had carried her through many experiences that to Hannah would have been embarrassing.

"How about coming upstairs, Debbie, and we'll discuss your art lesson today?" she asked. Once there, she intended to imprint on her a few facts of life. The lure of being able to extol the dreamy qualities of the fabulous Stan Bryant had never failed before, but today Debbie arched a dismissive eyebrow.

"Later, perhaps," she murmured. "Don't you think you'd better change if you plan to have lunch with us? I'm sure our guest has been embarrassed enough in seeing you looking so . . . disheveled." She wrinkled a dainty nose before fastening her entranced gaze once again on the strong features of the man beside her.

Hannah stilled the urge to box her sister's ears. She chewed her lower lip in vexation until she caught smoky eyes watching the action with what she could describe only as a hungry look. She gave up with a faint shrug and left the room in long graceful strides, all too aware that those same eyes were watching the undulation of her firm buttocks outlined by the brief shorts.

She let out her breath on reaching her room. She'd never been part of such an overt sensual encounter where, though not a word had been spoken, every nuance had been as explicit as if they had touched. She was glad of the cooling shower on her slightly feverish skin. Oh, my, yes, he was dangerous, she conceded, and her common sense warned that she should tread warily. But when she went through her wardrobe, she knew she was waiting expectantly for the next strangely exciting encounter.

She chose a white sundress that draped lovingly over the swell of her breasts and hugged her narrow waist. It was a perfect foil for the warm glow of her golden skin. She accented the slant to her almond-shaped eyes with kohl and glossed a coppery bronze on her lips. Clinky layers of gold bracelets lined her left arm and barbaric gold hoops swung from her ears. Her final act was to let a cloud of Havoc, her favorite perfume, settle over her.

"Well, Mr. Yale Upton," she said when she paused for a last check in the mirror, "let's see how you like the dressed version."

She had forgotten how his eyes could smoke their message of appreciation. He raised the glass of Scotch her father had poured in a silent toast before he took a sip.

She had to smile during the lunch at Debbie's maneuvers to vie for his attention. She was content to let the conversation flow around her, excitingly aware of how his gaze moved to her when hearing her bracelets tinkle. And when she did talk, his eyes fastened on the way the large earrings wavered in fleeting caresses against her slender neck.

From the conversation, she discovered he headed a firm named Upton Enterprises, and her father was acting as his lawyer while he was amalgamating with a smaller company.

"I understand from your father that you work for a head-hunting company," he said.

"We prefer to call it career matching," she returned dryly. "We're finding a large number of people are conceding that the rigors of the northern states are appalling and wish to relocate here in Florida. Why? Will you be needing our services now that you're enlarging your business?"

A faint smile moved his firm lips. "Yes, I might find that we'll need your services." The smile deepened when he saw she had caught the change in whom he liked the services to come from.

He left shortly thereafter and Hannah felt a vague sense of regret that the stimulating but dangerous game they had played was at an end.

CHAPTER TWO

"It's good to have you back, Hannah."

She looked up from the stack of files on her desk and gazed guardedly at the ruddy-faced man leaning nonchalantly against the door to her office. "Thanks, John, but I'm beginning to feel that when I'm through with all of these, I'll be needing another week off to recuperate."

"That's what you get for taking off for a month," he said in an attempt at humor. "You didn't see me give in to the flu for more than a week." A self-righteous look covered his face.

A flash of anger burst inside her. She'd been wondering how he'd act when she came back. She'd lashed him with caustic words when she'd finally struggled out of his embrace the last time she'd seen him. He hadn't come in the following day, calling in to say that he was bedridden with a 103 temperature. By that weekend she herself had succumbed to the flu bug he'd no doubt given her, and this was the first time they'd met since his ill-advised attempt at kissing her.

"I'd rather not talk about that exchange of viruses," she

said gloweringly. "But I want it made abundantly clear to you that if ever you attempt to repeat that episode, there'll be one less employee here as of that instant. There'll be no two-week notice while I break in a replacement. And I don't think Mr. Dunn will appreciate it when I tell him my reason for leaving."

He left the support of the door, the twitch to his shoulders hinting at his inner agitation. "Oh, for heaven's sake, Hannah, it was only a kiss. What's the big deal? You know you're a good looker, and you were giving me the bedroom eye . . ."

"Take a good look at these bedroom eyes!" she exploded.

He looked at her, startled by her vehemence, backing away on seeing the yellow shafts of anger blazing from them. She gave him time to become convinced that any seduction he thought he'd seen in their amber depths was a figment of his imagination.

"Let that be a notice of how I feel about any further amorous innuendos," she continued in a cold, measured voice. "And that includes the 'accidental' way you manage to touch me."

The air was electric between them, until she suddenly sagged back in her chair. Damn it, they had to work together and they couldn't the way they were glaring at each other now. "Look," she said, making a gargantuan effort to ease the tension. She was feeling guilty because she usually managed these confrontations better than this. She must still be more tired than she suspected. "Let's call a truce, John. We've worked together fairly well before this, and Mr. Dunn will soon know if things aren't going right at this end of the office. We have a job to do. Shall we say we both learned a lesson and go on from there?"

A look of grudging admiration touched his face. "I guess I stepped out of line," he admitted. "Let's say I tried and I don't have to be shot down twice to learn my lesson."

He came then to go over some of the client files with her, studiously careful that his arm didn't brush hers as was his habit.

The workload was heavy and Hannah had come in that Saturday morning to do the final catching up. She didn't mind, since her father had called to see if she'd be free for lunch that afternoon at his club. With Hannah back in her apartment, these Saturday lunch dates were one way they kept in touch.

While driving over to meet her father at his office, her mind wandered to the last client of the morning. She'd have to tell him subtly that if he thought that dying his hair made him appear younger, he should have professional consultation on the best color for his skin tone. His qualifications were excellent and she was certain they could place him, but he'd worked in a small family-owned company for fifteen years and had been untouched by the competition he had to face in today's market.

Hannah parked her car in the lot around the corner from her father's office in Palm Beach. She was halfway to his building when an unnoticed black cloud sent its load of water down in a blinding sheet of rain. It was typical of the mini-cloudbursts that peppered the subtropical area during the summer. Hannah muttered in disgust as she held her pocketbook protectively over her head and sprinted the last yards to the safety of the overhang. It turned into an irate shriek when a speeding car shot a sheet of dirty street water over her legs.

Lord, she was a sight, she groaned when stepping into the elevator that responded to her call. "For your edification, Dad," she said ruefully when marching into his office, "this drowned rat is your daughter!" She dug tissues from her purse and daubed ineffectually at the moisture dripping from her face. "And this time I can't blame it on Boston!"

"Here, let me." Her hands were brushed aside as a finger lifted her chin. She was held by smoky eyes bright with amusement as a large white handkerchief carefully blotted her face. "Remember, in Florida we call it heavy dew," Yale said casually. "It's why the women in England have such lovely skin." His finger slid along the curve of her flawless cheek, letting her know before his hand dropped away that its texture pleased him.

Hannah wavered a second as if off-balance, her body unaccountably tilting toward him. She blinked a few times to dispel the odd sensation of possession she'd felt under his ministrations.

"You are a mess!" Debbie said bluntly. "Couldn't you have waited in the car until it was over? You can't go to the Sailfish Club looking like that! You'll disgrace our guest."

Hannah arched an eyebrow at her sister's sharp denunciation. A pink-and-white confection in a crisp lawn dress that ruffled demurely around her neck and flared out from her narrow waist in a frothy fullness she'd moved over to Yale, a hand tucked possessively in his arm.

"Heaven forbid that I should cause anyone such discomfort!" Hannah said with mocking alarm. Her eyes were lit with amusement in recognition of her sister's act. Was she trying to establish territorial rights? Surely the little fool should see that no one, far less a woman, could hope to confine this man. He was a panther and needed unfettered space to roam in. If there was any possessing done, it would be by him and on his terms.

"Do you think you could manage sneaking a tray to me in the car?" she murmured, her expression one of crestfallen hope.

"In that case I'll have to share your banishment," Yale

said, his solemn expression marred by the minute twitch at the corner of his mouth. "We can't permit you to eat by yourself."

"I always believed that every dark cloud had its silver lining." She slanted amber cat's eyes at him and smiled beguilingly, hoping that he couldn't see how her pulse had leapt into high gear at the unexpected sight of him.

Her father gave her an indulgent look. "I'll give you five minutes to freshen up and then we'll be off."

She patted her sister on her curly-topped head before going to the lavatory. "Bear up, Debbie, I won't shame you!"

Debbie charmingly pouted and Hannah shook her head with amusement, wondering once again if the little vixen practiced before a mirror. She well remembered the confusion and conflicts of growing up and was thankful they were all behind her.

There was little she could do about her mud-splattered nylons, so she removed her panty hose and washed her legs, thankful that her enforced vacation had given her time to add to the tan. She brushed the escaped wisps of hair into place and retouched her lipstick.

While her hands were busy, her mind was racing with conflicting emotions. She'd accepted that the likelihood of ever seeing Yale again was minute, had in fact at last pushed that inflamatory meeting into a corner of her mind. But now he was back again and she realized with a shock that his imprint had remained indelible from the special way his mouth curved into a smile to the way he moved his long, tanned hands.

She took a deep breath and expelled it slowly before returning to the office, conscious of a recurrence of the excitement he seemed to trigger so easily.

As expected, the sun was shining brightly when they emerged from the building. The only signs of the short but heavy rain were the rapidly drying puddles. How typical of Florida, she mused. The rain could descend as if everyone had to take to the boats to survive, only to have it stop as abruptly as it had started, leaving the sun and sandy soil to eradicate quickly all evidence of its passing.

"Shall we join forces and take my car?" her father asked when they reached the parking lot.

"I'd better take mine, Wilson," Yale said. "I'll need it after lunch. Won't you join me?" he asked, taking Hannah's arm and ushering her into the seat of his copper red Porsche.

It was done smoothly, Hannah conceded with admiration at his maneuvering. She had a quick glimpse of Debbie flouncing into the Mercedes before Yale backed the car out of the parking space.

"That was done with great finesse and no doubt from long practice," she murmured with amusement.

He arched a sardonic look at her, not pretending that he didn't know what she was referring to. "It saves arguments," he admitted.

"Do you always get your way?" she asked, tilting her head to better examine his strong profile.

He stopped for a traffic light and turned to meet her examination. "Always," he admitted. "Let that be lesson number one to you, Ms. Hannah Blake." His smoky eyes rested on her curved lips and she was aghast over how they involuntarily softened and parted slightly.

"I'm not likely to be concerned over any such lesson," she returned, trying to hide her sudden breathlessness.

"Is that a challenge, Ms. Blake?" he asked silkily. "Lesson number two that you'll have to learn is that I never refuse a challenge."

"Of course not!" she said much too quickly, refusing to confess to an alarming sensation that she was about to step into quicksand and it was wise to backtrack quickly. Oh, yes, a dangerous man!

The impatient beep of the horn behind them warned that the traffic signal had changed. They left Worth Avenue, passed Flagler Bridge, which led to the mainland, and continued north on the narrow spit of high-priced real estate that was Palm Beach.

He turned the car in at the exclusive Sailfish Club, not far from the Lake Worth Inlet. The Mercedes pulled in next to them and the four of them entered the long, low, white building and were greeted warmly by the hostess. Occasionally Hannah and her father tried other various restaurants, but the consistently superlative food at the club made it their favorite choice.

They were led down the long corridor lined with an impressive number of silver cups won in past regattas to Hannah's and her father's usual table reserved by the window overlooking Lake Worth.

The wide body of water wasn't a true lake but rather a part of the intracoastal waterway that threaded its way down the eastern coast of the United States. It was the weekend and the water was filled with pleasure boats fishing as well as pulling water skiers. Hannah noticed that the club's small sailing dinghies were being prepared by the youthful members for the weekly race. How she loved this area! she thought with a happy sigh. She couldn't imagine living anyplace else.

"Have you ever been here for their Sunday night buffet dinners?" she asked Yale after the waitress handed them the menus. "Everyone goes into raptures over them," she added when he nodded his head.

"I've been to many other restaurants during my lifetime," her father said, "but none can touch what they put out at this club."

"I always end up with several desserts," Debbie giggled, her delight slipping through her guard.

Hannah regarded her with affection. How valiantly she was trying to appear the sophisticate before their worldly guest! She'd love to inform her she'd be infinitely more appealing if she'd simply act her age, but knew the poor girl would suspect her reason, especially after Yale had singled her out to ride in his car. With Debbie poised at the edge of young womanhood, she hoped to prevent any jealousy occurring between them over male friends. Debbie must be made to believe with certainty that her more mature sister would never compete with her.

A smile twitched Hannah's lips. What foolish nonsense was she thinking! She was ten years older than Debbie. Her sister's boyfriends were immature neophytes in her eyes. As for Yale, no one could hope to dissuade him from whoever caught his attention. He'd already warned her with his so-called lesson. He'd make certain he got his own way. Always. And she had no doubt that it was true whether it was in business or with a woman.

He lifted his water glass and she marveled at the hidden strength his hand projected. His face had indicated that same controlled power and her gaze went to follow the line of the slightly jutting jaw and over the almost black hair cut fashionably to just below his ears. In her imagination she could feel its vibrant life under her hands and it shocked her over the wayward path her thoughts had taken her. Her eyes moved to his to see if he was aware of her evaluation.

Smoky eyes met hers, laughing knowingly, as if he'd been following her every thought. It took a concentrated effort on Hannah's part to meet them coolly and not to drop her gaze in embarrassment. A woman would be wise not to think she could take this one on carelessly, she warned herself. He'd always be one step ahead of her!

"I was going to ask if you'd want a game of tennis tomorrow, Hannah," her father said when they contemplated the tempting desserts rolled to them on a cart for their inspection. "But you don't look like you're fully over the effects of that bug as yet. Have they been working you too hard?" A concerned frown creased his brow as he checked the faint shadow under her eyes.

"I've been away from my desk almost a month," she reminded him. "But don't fret, love, I'm doing okay. If you're free next week, I'll take you on." While their love was deep, they both respected each other's need for a private life. Her father was still comparatively young and devastatingly handsome with his thick shock of tawny hair only lightly streaked with the first signs of silver. He was bound to want the companionship of women; in fact, she'd been introduced to several.

As for herself—her eyes darkened with remembered pain—she'd been wildly in love in her senior year in college. It was only on graduation that she'd found that the engagement had been a convenience used by her fiancé to bring her to his bed. She'd been devastated to find out that hadn't been enough, that Jim had also been indulging in a variety of favors on the side. It had taken a long time to get over that discovery, and she still looked at any confession of deep affection with a jaundiced eye. The duplicity had scarred her deeply. At the least, she'd learned to be very selective. It had been a difficult way to mature, but she'd learned her lesson well.

"Then we have a date for tomorrow at eight," her father said, and Hannah realized during her daydreaming he and Yale had agreed to a match the following day. In her mind's eye she could see him in tennis shorts, the play of muscles on his long bronze legs as he chased the ball. He'd be superb, she knew instinctively, and reached for her coffee cup to moisten her suddenly dry mouth.

Seeing Debbie's indecision, her father turned to assist her in her selection of desserts from the trolley.

"I wonder what's going through your mind right now," Yale murmured softly to Hannah as he leaned toward her. "Such slumberous cat's eyes that promise such pleasures. If I stroke you, will you purr?"

"I'd no doubt hiss and show my claws," she returned smartly. Good Lord, were none of her thoughts private from him?

"But only in the beginning," he returned with supreme masculine assurance. "It will make the purring more of a delight."

"What are your plans for this afternoon?" she asked, turning resolutely to her sister.

"I'm sort of free," Debbie said, raising wide blue eyes hopefully to Yale. "I bought a new bikini and thought I'd go to the beach."

Hannah's lips thinned for a second. Did Debbie think seeing her in a bikini would lure this man? He could visually strip a woman bundled in a snowsuit and still know every curve intimately.

"I wish I could join you, but I haven't had time as yet to fully restock my apartment after closing it. As soon as Dad takes us back I'll pick up my car and get my marketing done."

It didn't work out quite that way. As they were leaving, a business friend struck up a conversation with her father and while they were talking, their young son fastened his attention on Debbie. She flirted outrageously with the boy while keeping one eye on Yale to see how he was reacting.

"This could go on for a while," Hannah explained ruefully to Yale. "Mr. Johnson loves to hear the sound of his own voice, and once he's cornered someone, they're trapped for half an hour."

"Then I'll make our excuses and take you back," he

said, and did so before Hannah could prevent him. In the close confines of his sports car she was again assailed by the sensations he stirred in her that were composed of an equal mixture of a warning excitement and an odd sense of anticipation.

"Which market do you shop in?" he asked, and when she told him, she was surprised when he took her to it.

"I have to pick up some things also," he said blandly as he held the door open for her.

It was a new experience shopping with a man. She had thought he was playing some game with her, but on seeing him carefully evaluate the relative merits of two labels, she concluded he'd done it before.

He stacked the bundles in the trunk and drove her to where her car was parked. She started to transfer the bags when he took the keys from her hand and unlocked her door.

"Get in," he ordered. "No use wasting time changing them here. I'll follow you to your place."

Alarm bells rang and she stiffened in rebellion. If he noticed, he gave no sign. She was in the car, the key in the ignition, and the door closed firmly behind her. She sputtered impotently as he gave a cheery wave through the closed window and returned to his Porsche. If he thought his maneuvering was going to give him an entry to her apartment, he had another think coming, she glowered vehemently as she ground the car out of the parking lot. He was traveling too fast for her. She preferred to keep the pace of any relationship under her firm control.

She should have known her protestations would be ignored, she admitted ruefully when later he deposited the filled bags on the counter in her kitchen. How did he do it? she wondered, slightly dazed by his tactics. Was this how he'd built his electronics company from its modest beginnings?

From what she'd overheard of his conversations with her father, he was a self-made man. Maybe not a millionaire as yet, but with the new acquisition, close enough so it made little difference.

"Better put away what has to go in the refrigerator," he warned. He had the cupboards open and with an alarmingly discerning eye seemed to know the correct places for the various food items.

She pulled out a large steak and stared at it in surprise. She'd never bought it; it must have been placed in her package by mistake. "That's for tonight," he informed her as he reached to place a box of cereal on an upper shelf.

"Tonight!" she cried, unable to believe she had heard him correctly.

"Yes," he said agreeably as he set the cans of fruit in an orderly row. "The beach your sister mentioned didn't appeal to me, but I thought a sail in my boat would be the thing." He turned to her and stared into her face. "I don't like those shadows your father noticed. There's nothing more relaxing than a quiet sail on the lake. The wind isn't high and it might just lull you to sleep." A finger moved over the faint lavender circles under her eyes and then over her lips, slightly parted in reaction over his audacious assumptions.

"After being out on the water I always have a ravenous appetite," he continued, ignoring the warning sparks that were beginning to build in her eyes. "I thought we'd come back and have the steak. You don't have another date, do you?" he asked as an afterthought.

"No . . . yes!" She was shouting as if the volume would help her words to penetrate his overdeveloped ego. How dare he walk into her apartment and think he could rearrange her day!

A complacent smile curved his lips. "I'm glad you

don't. No need to cause any problems this early with any of your boyfriends."

She drew herself up to her full five feet ten and still had to look up as she prepared to cut a few ribbons of flesh from his tough hide. "I have no intention of going anywhere with you this afternoon . . . or ever!" she began haughtily.

"Hush, Hannah," he said benignly. "Run off and put on something light. A bikini would be nice, or that ever so fetching yellow outfit you wore the first time we met. Perhaps I can stir up some spray so it can produce the same effect."

In spite of herself, Hannah had to smile, if somewhat grimly. She remembered all too well how the damp material of the thin cotton halter had been molded to her.

"You," she said succinctly, "can take a long walk off a short pier! I have no intention of going anyplace with you."

He gave a small sigh before taking a step toward her. "Have you already forgotten the two lessons I gave you?"

The question was asked softly, but Hannah found herself licking her lips nervously. The admonition was explicit, the sugar coating not hiding the warning being issued.

"Be a good girl and do as I say," he continued, stopping inches from her. "Wilson said you love sailing and I've been too busy lately to go out. It will do us both good."

Something warned Hannah she daren't give in. His conceit was formidable and she'd be damned if she'd let him order her around. To do so now would be to lose whatever control she had over their relationship.

"Hannah"—his voice was a mere whisper—"I'm giving you fifteen minutes to change. If necessary, I'll be only to glad to do it for you. Of course, I might have lost interest in sailing by then."

He better not be laughing at me! she stormed on finding

herself in her bedroom. Bikini, hah! She'd be a fool to expose that much of her body to his evaluating eye. She selected the only one-piece suit she owned and defiantly buttoned a cotton beach jacket to her neck before presenting herself to the arrogant man.

His eyes lingered with male satisfaction on the expanse of long, slender legs exposed beneath the jacket and she berated herself for not dressing in a long beach robe. "Just as perfect as I remembered," he said approvingly. "I'm glad to see my memory hasn't played tricks."

The statement sounded almost clinical. There was nothing leering in his words, and Hannah was suddenly extremely happy that her legs were in perfect proportion and the golden tan she'd acquired showed them off to excellent advantage.

"Where is this boat you promised?" she asked jauntily, stuffing a beach towel into a carryall. She'd never yet been on a sail without being hit by some spray and it was wise to be prepared.

"On the mainland," he said as he waited for her to lock her door. "I called while you were changing to have them put some ice and soda on board. I always get thirsty when on the water."

"Me too," she admitted. "And I can't figure out why."

They crossed Flagler Bridge and turned north to the Palm Beach Yacht Club. She discovered he owned a twenty-two-foot catboat which she knew drew about eighteen inches with the center board up, the shallow draft ideal for Lake Worth with its many shoaling areas.

"It will be high tide shortly," he said after consulting with the dock tender. "We should be able to skim over the thin spots with no trouble."

He jumped on board and shortened the line while offering his hand to steady her leap. "You can stow your gear below," he said, unlocking the hatch to the cuddy cabin and pulling out the sail bags.

She peered into the shadowy depths when tossing in the carryall. As with all catboats, the head room was limited. She, and certainly Yale, would have to crouch on entering. But the beauty of the make was its broad beam and stability. She wasn't surprised to see a basic galley on one side and an exceptionally wide bunk on the other. Large enough for two, and she had an instant vision of two people sleeping there, arms entwined, one dark-haired and the other . . . ?

"Do you take many weekend trips?" she asked, brushing her hair back with suddenly nervous fingers. She was thankful he was concentrating on fastening the large sail to the mast and didn't see her uncharacteristic agitation. With his disturbing ability to walk into her mind, he'd be certain to see the aftervision still imprinted there.

"Not as many as I'd like. Why, would you like to come on one?" Smoky eyes touched hers briefly before returning to his job.

"Hardly," she said primly. "Besides, you've only one bunk."

He gave her a devil's smile. "Noticed that, did you? Then you saw that it's wide enough to accommodate two."

She looked at the broad expanse of shoulders. "I doubt it with you in it," she returned dryly. "There'd be no sleeping for anyone else with you taking up all the room."

"How right you are. But then sleep could be the last thing occupying my mind."

This time he saw her lips flatten into a thin line and he grinned widely. "You asked for that, Ms. Blake. Now be a good mate and help me bend the sail."

She worked smoothly with him, feeding him the clips as she pulled the huge sail out of the bag so he could fasten it to the mast and then the boom. He then went below in the cabin and handed out the cushions for the comfortably wide cockpit seats.

When he emerged he was in black swim trunks and the sudden sight of his bronze nakedness sent Hannah's senses into a tailspin. Her hand went involuntarily over her heart to still its wild beat. Oh, my God, no man should be allowed to be so blatantly gorgeous!

"All set?" he asked while scanning the sky with a practiced eye. "There are few clouds today. Will you need a sunscreen when you finally decide to remove that damned jacket?" A black brow rose in quiet derision over her high-buttoned covering.

"I was simply waiting for you to finish in the cabin," she returned with a sniff. "And, no, I don't need a lotion. I don't burn." She held her back stiffly to him while she undid the large buttons. When leaning into the hatch to toss the jacket onto the bunk, the hot sun on her back made her remember that while the front of the suit fit demurely, the cut was such that the sides and back were free to the warm rays.

His gaze smoked over her in open admiration. "Very sassy," he commented before turning his attention to unfastening the restraining lines. The small engine caught and he steered the boat from the dock and out of the marked channel of the Intracoastal Waterway.

"We'll stay in the shallower areas. I don't want to dodge the big boats," he said, surrendering the tiller to Hannah while he hoisted the outsize sail into position and tied down the halyard.

It was a dreamy afternoon. He tossed her a small cushion for her head when her eyes became heavy under the soothing sounds of water slapping against the hull and the warm breeze ruffling her hair with tender fingers. "Take a nap," he said. "We're on a long reach and the sail will keep the sun off you most of the way."

She had no intention of obeying, but she woke with a start when the boat tilted at the opposite angle as he went on a different tack.

"Want me to spell you for a while?" she asked. If she didn't do something, she'd fall asleep again and she had the definite sensation that his gaze had roamed as frequently over her body as over the water.

"Get some soda from the cooler first," he ordered. "I'll show you her little idiosyncrasies then. Like all females, she likes to show spurts of independence, but once you know what they are, she's easy to handle."

She let her withering look be her answer, and he was still chuckling when she returned with the cold drinks. She sat opposite him and he gave her the tiller, letting her feel the boat's reaction as he pointed out what to stay alert to. "A catboat's sail is tremendous for its size, and, for heaven's sake, never stand up when you change tack or the boom could well decapitate you! She's a tender little lady and responds very quickly to the tiller, so don't overcompensate when you do any dodging."

He checked her handling of the boat while finishing his drink, then stood up and stretched, sending her body into a convoluting reaction on seeing the play of muscles under taut skin.

"How do you describe your hair?" he asked with lazy interest.

"Mottled." Her lips quirked on seeing his brow arch with amusement. "It's every shade from blond to brown. Someday I'll have it bleached so I'll know what color to name it."

"No!" he said forcefully, reaching to lift a strand and let it filter slowly through his fingers. "Most definitely no. It belongs with your personality." His gaze moved slowly over her face. "Always different, always intriguing, changing even as one looks at it."

The sail snapped as it luffed, dragging her attention back to the course. He had no right doing that to her, distracting her so she almost spilled the air out of the sails.

He settled into position on the cushions she had just vacated. "Happy?" he asked softly.

A quick smile lit her face as she nodded in response. She *was* happy. Comfortably, deliciously happy. It was a sensation quite unlike any she'd ever experienced before, and she wished that the afternoon could go on forever.

"You look like you belong there." His eyes were heavy, his voice sleepy. "Yes, we definitely will have to have that weekend," he murmured as if answering a private question. His black lashes lowered, and it took a major effort for Hannah to tear her gaze from him. The sunny weather was bringing out many boaters and she didn't dare indulge in a long examination, no matter how hungry her senses were clamoring for gratification.

He woke finally when a passing speedboat created a tumultuous wake, causing the sail to flap loudly in protest as it was forced to dump its air. He raised his head to check their position and smiled lazily at her as he stretched once more before sitting up.

He must know what he's doing to me, she thought somewhat wildly as her hands showed white knuckles on the tiller. "Do you think we can drop anchor and take a swim?" she asked, hoping her voice didn't sound quite as strangled as she feared it did. She had to do something to temper the heat waves setting her on fire.

"A good idea," he said. "Head for Peanut Island. It's close enough to the inlet so we'll have the fresher ocean water to swim in."

She sailed past the white buildings of the Coast Guard station situated on the wooded island and headed the boat into the wind to ease the tension on the huge sail while Yale undid the halyard to let it drop. The anchor went over next, and when he was satisfied it was holding snugly, he went below to dig out a boarding ladder from one of the lockers.

The water was delightfully refreshing. Hannah porpoised like a playful sea pup, the previous happiness returning as the inner turmoil subsided. When Yale dived repeatedly under the boat to check if the bottom paint was keeping the barnacles and weeds at bay, she was beside him, assisting in the inspection.

"Looks like it will hold up for another month or two," he said, tossing his water-logged hair out of his eyes. "Come, mermaid, one more lap around the boat and we'd better think about heading back."

They matched a lazy crawl until they reached the ladder. "Not so fast," he murmured when she grasped the handles to heave herself up. She was rotated in position until she was facing him and found herself cradled in the circle of his arms while he steadied them both with his grasp on the ladder.

At last! It came as a silent sigh, and she knew this was what she'd been hoping for, waiting for. Her lips parted slightly in expectation. His mouth was firm and cool and tasted of the salt water they'd been swimming in.

"Mmm, nice," he growled deep in his throat. "Now get up on deck so I can do a decent job of this."

She was propelled up the ladder with him following quickly behind her. When she reached for her towel he pulled it away and tossed it on the cushions.

"No," he said somewhat fiercely. "I want you wet and cool in my arms. I want to feel the heat build up and see the steam rise from you!"

Her eyes held startled amusement at his audacious words and the picture they evoked. Then she was pulled into his arms and his mouth took possession of hers in a hungry kiss that had her helplessly drowning in a maelstrom of sensations such as she'd never encountered before. His hands moved restlessly over the bare skin of her back and she found herself doing the same in her need to feel every muscle, every indentation of his back's wonderful expanse.

"Very definitely steaming," he said huskily when the necessity to breathe made him tear his mouth from hers.

She shrank against him when shrill whistles reached them from a passing speedboat. The grinning occupants gave the A-okay sign as they sped on their way.

"Jealous," he muttered with a grin that dismissed them. He lowered her to the cushions where the sides of the cockpit acted as a partial screen. His first hungry demand had been met and now the kiss was a drugging seduction. His hands, as if satisfied with their first urgent search, moved in smooth caresses over her arms, down her rib cage and circled warmly over her flat abdomen.

When his mouth moved over the moist skin of her throat, her eyes drifted open to see that the gentle rocking from the waves moved the mast in lazy circles as it pointed to the cloudless blue sky. *This is a dream,* she mused, and prayed fervently that she wouldn't awaken for hours.

His fingers gave a tug on the thin straps of her swimsuit and the top was pulled down to expose her full, aching breasts. "Oh, God, you're beautiful," he groaned as he buried his face in their valley. His hand cupped one, roughing the peak with his thumb while his mouth closed hungrily over its twin.

The yearning that had started hours before deep within her became an avalanche of desire that swept away all coherent thought. She writhed on the cushions, his name a litany on her lips. "Yale . . . please . . . oh, Yale!"

A strong tremor ran through him before he raised his

head to gaze deeply into her passion-drugged eyes. "I want you, too, sweet one," he husked, "but not here. I forgot to open the forward hatch, and it's an oven below."

A sigh of acceptance escaped her lips. She had been quick to leave the cabin's heat before when getting the sodas and knew it would be intolerable there now.

He placed a last kiss on each hard peak before replacing the suit top with great reluctance. He then rose swiftly and arched into a dive into the water.

Hannah felt too weak to follow. She lay still, staring dazedly at the lazily circling mast top, unable to marshal her thoughts into any order. Her aroused emotions still held sway, and they were crying in outrage at the abrupt cessation of their seduction. Finally, with a moan, she curled into the hard back of the seat in an attempt to blot out the world and the rioting memories.

Cool lips touched her nape. "If it helps any, I'm in bad shape too," Yale said, rolling her gently on her back. She saw the rueful smile on his lips before they met hers in a light, passionless kiss that somehow banked the fires into a controllable glow.

"I never meant it to get so out of hand," he admitted. His tender fingers brushed her tawny hair from her forehead before he gathered her into a protective embrace. Her head was held against the curly hairs of his water-cooled chest and she lay there, comforted by the steady beat of his heart under her ear.

"It's getting late, pretty one. We'd better pull up the anchor." He placed a kiss on her forehead after giving her a last searching glance. They then busied themselves raising the anchor and hoisting the sail in preparation for the trip back to the dock.

The late afternoon breeze was strong from the southeast and they had an exhilarating race back, rail down all the way. The dock tender caught their line and after seeing to the fastening of the boat Hannah found herself humming happily as she assisted Yale in unhooking the sail and holding the bag as he stuffed it inside.

He held her jacket for her, then turned her to fasten the large buttons down its front. Their eyes held for a long, breathless minute before he bent to place a kiss on her soft lips.

"That wasn't so bad, was it?" he asked teasingly. "I've returned you slightly damp but otherwise unchanged."

Unchanged! She had to swallow a hysterical laugh. He'd sent her into orbit around the earth and he thought she was unchanged! She had a horrible conviction she'd never be the same again. And for a fleeting moment, Hannah was confused by a deep sense of fear.

CHAPTER THREE

"I," Yale said, placing his clothes into the trunk of his car, "am starving. That steak is more tempting every minute."

She glanced at him as he backed the car from its parking place. They had on their now dry swimsuits, but he'd pulled on a T-shirt that he'd found in the boat. The way it outlined his torso made her hands tingle with memories.

When they reached the apartment he pushed her toward the bathroom, telling her to take her shower while he prepared a drink. She had hurriedly complied, fearful that he'd follow her, and perversely irritated when he didn't. Was it all part of his plan to keep her off-base and wondering over his next move?

Her doubts solidified when, on entering her bedroom, one towel tucked around her and another in use to towel her hair dry, she found him reclining on her bed.

"What are you doing in here?" she said frostily. She might have been putty in his hands that afternoon, but that weakness had passed and she was in control of herself.

"Jes' bringin' in yoah drink, Ms. Blake," he said meekly, pointing to where a glass sat on her dresser, a coaster placed carefully underneath to catch the moisture pearling on its iced sides.

He levered himself pantherlike from the bed and scooped up his clothes as he headed for the shower. "I hope you have decent size towels," he said meaningfully.

She glowered at him. He was an extra large man and would need them, but then she liked them herself. "Yes," she clipped. "In fact, you'll find two on the stool if it pleases your lordship."

He paused by the bathroom door to gaze back at her. It was impossible, but she was certain she could smell the smoke coming from his eyes! "I like proper acquiescence, my dear, but watch your tone! And what pleases me is that you've a queen-size bed. We're tall people, Hannah, and I'm happy to see that you, too, like your comfort."

Her mouth gaped as he disappeared into the shower stall, not bothering to close the door, so she could hear him whistling as he soaped himself.

The nerve! The arrogance! The insufferable boor! Her hand trembled as she reached for the glass and gulped down half of the contents before realizing its strength. Her eyes watered as the heat hit her stomach. It had nothing to do with the steam sending up her blood pressure. So he was attempting to get her drunk to further his nefarious seduction, was he? Did he think her a child to be taken in by such crude tricks?

She had a sudden and overwhelming desire to trap him in a snare of her own making. The initiative had been too long in his hands. She spent a thoughtful minute going over her clothes before making her selection. Yale would have been immediately on guard if he'd seen the gleam in her eyes.

She had worn the flowing caftan she now donned often when she entertained at home. Only before, Hannah had worn underwear, because the material was more translucent than opaque. When it brushed against her body a discerning eye would soon see that she was *sans* undergarments. And Yale had, if nothing else, extremely discerning eyes. She'd feed him his steak, then send him sizzling on his way. Get her tipsy, would he? She'd show him who seduced whom only to be left panting from frustration!

She was blow-drying her hair when he emerged from the bathroom. She smiled sweetly from beneath the curtain her hair afforded but didn't catch the way his hands clenched involuntarily on seeing the tawny cloud billowing gently in all its silken splendor.

He reached for the glass he'd set on the night table and did a remarkable imitation of the way Hannah had just gulped half her drink. His face twisted in a grimace as he stared at the contents, then went to her to exchange the glasses.

"I must have given you mine by mistake," he said, then paused in surprise on seeing her partially drained glass. "I had assumed that you wouldn't like it as strong as I did, but I see I made a mistake."

He would never know the rush of relief that swept through her at his confession. She should have known he was above such crass tactics! "I was about to add some water to it," she admitted in a small voice that had him regarding her with piercing interest.

She hurriedly bent her head to brush her now dry hair. He took the brush from her hand and she met his eyes in the mirror as he wielded it in slow strokes. It was a new exercise in seduction that had her quivering by the time he was finished.

Her lips were parted in throbbing anticipation when he drew her from her seat. He looked undecided for a moment before he turned her to the door and gave a smart tap to her derrière. "Temptress," he growled, "get to the kitchen. I took the steak out of the refrigerator and it's ready for the broiler. It would be wise to feed me."

She gave him an outraged look on hearing his knowing chuckle and flounced to the kitchen. She hoped he liked his steak burned to a crisp, because that was how he was going to get it!

It wasn't, of course. It was served juicy and tender with a tossed salad and thick chunks of hot Italian bread dripping with garlic butter. She remembered the bottles of rosé she'd buried deep in a closet for a special occasion, and rescued one. What more special occasion could she wish for than sharing a meal with an utterly charming man who, while conversing on many subjects, was letting it be known he found his companion most alluring.

It was a rapturous meal, aided no doubt by the admitted light-headedness started by that first incautious downing of potent scotch.

The second bottle of wine was upended by the time Hannah rose to plug in the coffeemaker. She clutched the back of her chair and blinked in an attempt to still the sudden tilting of the room. Oh, dear, she groaned inwardly, the sly vixen had been outfoxed! She was properly smashed. A giggle escaped before she could stop it. It wouldn't do to let panther man see her condition. He'd pounce and drag her to his lair, which, on second thought, might not be such a bad idea, she decided with bleary acceptance. The giggle escaped again.

Massive shoulders blocked her view and strong arms encircled her loosely to give her balance. "My God," he said with a smothered laugh, "a twenty-seven-year-old neophyte! I didn't know you couldn't handle the wine or I'd have rationed you."

She stared in fascination at his mouth. She'd never seen one before with a third lip. Strange that it didn't repel her, but she did wonder how he managed to kiss with that anomaly. The thought suddenly flustered her and she dropped her eyes to concentrate on the delightfully curly hair exposed by the partially open shirt. A girl could go crazy running her hands through it, she decided, moving a finger to test its texture.

The broad chest expanded in a sudden inhalation. "Hannah," he said in a tight voice. "This might sound silly, but have you ever slept with a man?"

She stiffened even as she gazed with owlish concentration at her wayward finger. "I was engaged," she said with careful enunciation. "He said it made it legal. He got me in bed three times before it blew up. One, two, three times." She poked in emphasis at his chest with three successive fingers. "Wam, bam, thank you, ma'am. And you know what? The whole scene is for the birds . . . no, it's rabbits, isn't it?" A hiccup escaped even as she brushed at the wet trail made by a tear.

His arms tensed for a second before relaxing again. "And have there been any men since?" he asked softly.

She shook her head before stilling the violent movement and squeezed her eyes shut until the room stopped its dizzying rotation. "Dontcha know, I'm a quick learner? Who needs that kind of hashh . . . hassle." She peered cautiously at the mouth to see how the three lips were doing before attempting to look at his eyes. If she found three there, she'd collapse. Satisfied that there were the accepted two, she leaned closer to whisper, "And do you know what? Some of my boyfriends shay . . . say I'm frigid. Whaddo you think about that!"

Yale placed a finger against her lower lip to still its trembling. "I'd say they were damned liars," he muttered, barely able to keep the anger from showing.

She placed her head trustingly in the warm curve of his neck. "Thank you," she murmured, giving a big yawn. "I believe you."

He held her gently in his arms for a long minute before she raised a sleepy head. "Are you going to prove you're right?" she asked with abstract interest.

He shook his head as he gave a rueful laugh. "You're beyond too much, you crazy woman. No, I'm not going to prove anything tonight. And you can stop looking at me with those bedroom eyes that are begging for trouble. I'll do all the proving you want at another time, and I'll make damned certain you've not had a drink in you, so you'll never forget how you can respond to a man."

She nodded in complacent acceptance, causing his chest to rumble with a low chuckle. Hannah was swept into his arms and carried to the bedroom. She was asleep almost before he pulled the covers over her after depositing her on the bed.

She woke up from a dream in which she was on a desert and was dying of thirst, her mouth stuffed with cotton balls. She finally opened her eyes to shut them immediately, fighting the sudden heave in her stomach. She raised trembling fingers to press them against her throbbing temples. Oh, God, she wanted to die!

She lay perfectly still until she felt it was safe to open her eyes again. It was a long time since she'd been foolish enough to overindulge enough to suffer a hangover. In fact, the last time had been when in college. She'd discovered early that she disliked the sensation of losing control of herself and became a selective drinker.

What had made her do otherwise last night? she wondered painfully as she rose to sit cautiously at the edge of the bed. She had rescued the second bottle of wine from its hiding place with scarcely a thought when the first one had been emptied. True, she'd been entranced by the scope of subjects they'd covered. They'd laughed, they'd argued amiably, had even bared some inner thoughts never before shared. She groaned in disgust at herself. It had been a magic night and she'd ruined it by getting herself bombed.

Not until the stinging spray under the shower had cleared away the remaining cobwebs did she recall those last minutes before she'd fallen asleep. Had she really spoken those words? she wondered in dismay. Surely she was still befuddled and they were simply part of the murky dreams that had invaded her sleep! She was begging herself to believe it true, but when she was forced to look at herself in the mirror while brushing her teeth, she had to admit it had really happened.

How could she have acted so sickening! No man as mature as Yale would be interested in following that type of confession with future dates. How often did a woman have the chance to meet such a fascinating man? He had irritated even as he intrigued. They'd shared warm laughter and sharp debates, and under it all had been the exciting awareness and she'd ruined it with her childish display at the end.

On reaching the kitchen she was amazed to discover he'd cleaned away the remnants of their dinner and had stacked the plates in the dishwasher. She sipped black coffee in silent musing. The dull ache in her was, she knew, from regret. Yale had caught her attention like no other man, and it was all over before it had really begun.

She threw herself into cleaning her apartment. It hadn't had a thorough going-over since her illness and it gave her an excuse for staying at home in spite of the beautiful day outside. She couldn't still the shaft of anticipation whenever the phone rang, or the terrible letdown when the voice wasn't the deep purr she'd been hoping for.

This has to stop, she scolded herself, and pushed herself hard at work the following week so that when she collapsed in bed at night, she fell asleep from exhaustion. She blocked with firm determination all memory of fingers that left tingling trails over her body, of lips that seared with their brand of fire, and of gray eyes that watched her with smoky intensity.

When the weekend loomed before her, she was happy to accept an invitation from Ted Watson, an on-and-off boyfriend since high school days. It was for water skiing in the afternoon and to a dinner-dance being held that evening at the Breakers, the handsome grande dame of hotels in Palm Beach, facing the ocean.

"It's a charity thing," he confessed on picking her up in his HRG sports car. "I guess most of Palm Beach got snagged into attending. We should see some of the old crowd there."

"I can see why you're still not married," Hannah grimaced as the fetching custom-built but virtually springless car hit a rough spot in the road. "A prolonged ride in this would cause any young thing to have second thoughts."

"You'd be surprised how the opposite is true," he grinned. "How many cars do you know that have its hood belted down? It's very impressive when I undo the strap to show off the motor."

Hannah rolled up her eyes. "Everyone has their little quirks, I guess," she said dryly. "But next time remind me to bring along a cushion."

Another couple was waiting for them—Sue and Paul. They had a great time skimming the surface of Lake Worth, taking turns skiing behind Ted's new Chris Craft.

Hannah had always had an easy relationship with him, dating casually when he was between girl friends. They'd enjoyed many of the same things and could relax together, knowing nothing serious would ever develop between them. "You use me as a fuel stop," she'd teased him once, and surprisingly he'd agreed.

They had been on the beach and he'd been bemoaning the merry chase his last amour had led him. "You're good for a man's ego," he'd said. "He's damned glad to have such a good-looking woman with him so the other guys are a tinge jealous, yet you're emotionally undemanding to frayed nerves. Though I'll bet you can play havoc with dates if you're so inclined," he'd added magnanimously.

"Rat," she had laughed, further tousling his heavy shock of blond hair. He had a safe job in his father's brokerage firm and she imagined that was as far as his ambition would take him, but she liked his amiable personality.

He dropped her off at the apartment early enough to give her time to shampoo the salt out of her hair and dress appropriately for the night's activities.

She selected a white jersey dress, the bodice stitched completely in white silk embroidery. Spaghetti straps held it up and the front plunged just enough to make masculine eyes long for more. Multiple mock belts of the same spaghetti straps were tied in small bows at the narrow waist while the circular skirt fell in rich folds.

The afternoon sun had added depth to her golden tan. A touch of green eye shadow to her slanting eyes and a tawny rose lipgloss was all the makeup required. She added pearl earrings dangling on long chains and a large baroque pearl dinner ring.

Ted gave an appreciative whistle between his teeth when picking her up. "My gawd, woman, you get more stunning every time I see you. I don't know why I fool around and don't settle for you."

"I don't know why either," she said lightly as she checked her beaded bag to see if it held her key. "In fact," she said later when they were ushered to their table, "I've been wondering when you were going to tell me all about the trials and tribulations of your last affair." She didn't mind his unburdening. In fact, she enjoyed hearing about the ups and downs of his romances. He never went into intimate details, but what he did tell was frequently hilarious as he'd relate the faux pas committed by his good-natured bumbling.

He was silent so long that Hannah looked at him in surprise. His gentle eyes held a lost look and she could see the underlying pain.

"Hey, what gives, lover boy?" she asked softly. He winced and her hand went consolingly over his large square hand resting on the table. He was hurting, and she knew instinctively whoever his latest was, she had meant more than any of his past attachments. Had love finally caught up with her shaggy-haired friend?

"Tell me about her," she said sympathetically.

He gave a shrug of hopeless resignation. "What's to say? Ivy's the loveliest thing ever dreamed of. She's small, she's fragile, and when I'm with her, I feel so clumsy and afraid that she'll break if I'm not careful. I want to wrap her in the softest of silk and protect her from the world. And I thought she returned some of my feelings."

"What happened?" Hannah urged as he paused to stare moodily at his wineglass.

"A gang of us were invited to the house of one of her neighbors last week. They had a new stereo and we were dancing on the patio. Do you remember Stella Moore?" he asked sharply.

Hannah nodded. Who didn't know Stella! The self-proclaimed femme fatale with a reputation to match.

"She was there. She's in the process of divorcing her third or fourth husband, and for some unknown reason decided to latch on to me." Ted gave a bewildered shake to his head. "Why me, I don't know. I never gave her a tumble before."

"Maybe that's why," Hannah said dryly, and, on seeing his blank look, patted his hand absently. Some men would never understand the female mind.

"Anyway, when I went to the kitchen to fill the ice bucket, Stella followed me. Before I knew what hit me, she was all over me, and kissing me. She even had her leg wrapped around mine, and I couldn't get untangled."

Hannah hurriedly stilled the laughter bubbling in her as her imagination pictured the scene. "You don't have to tell me the rest," she said knowingly. "Ivy came in and saw it all."

He nodded gloomily. "She won't answer my phone calls and when I went to her house her mother said she wasn't in, though I know she was."

"Give it time," Hannah said. What else could she say? "She'll get over it."

"Yeah," he said, the single word telling of his disbelief. He gulped down his glass of wine, then forced a smile. "End of the sad tale of Ted Watson. I'm with the best-looking woman here, and I'm being the fool to let my problems take over."

He launched with hearty intensity into the trials and tribulations of owning a foreign sports car that was no longer in production.

The dining room was filling rapidly with the glittering elite that was Palm Beach. As Ted had predicted, they saw many mutual friends and most stopped to exchange some gossip before going to their own tables. Ted evidently wasn't up to an evening of social chitchat and had managed to commandeer one of the few tables for two, which gave her an idea of the extent of his desolation. Whoever Ivy was, she had dealt him a lethal blow. She was truly sorry for her bulky escort and hoped the two would soon iron out their differences.

"Does your neck bother you?" he asked solicitously. "You've been rubbing it for the past fifteen minutes."

Hannah halted her hand in the act of massaging the back of her neck.

"I wasn't aware of it," she said in some surprise. "I guess I pulled something when water skiing." She realized she felt no pain but rather a sense of pressure.

Ted's gaze drifted around the room and suddenly he stiffened. "She's here!" he hissed. He half-rose from his chair before sagging back into it.

Hannah stilled the urge to look around. She didn't have to ask who he meant. The swift flood of joy to his face told its story. Her old friend was really smitten.

"She's with her parents and another man." His face seemed to age as he spoke. "No wonder she doesn't answer my calls if she has that black-haired bastard dancing attendance," he said bitterly.

Hannah took in his unhappy expression and wondered about a way to end the impasse. Perhaps she could urge him to walk casually past Ivy's table and stop to talk. "Has she seen you?" she asked gently.

"Oh, yes," he answered with an abrupt laugh. "And if icy stares could kill, I'd be flat on the floor."

Hannah rubbed the back of her neck thoughtfully, wondering what to do to help her hurting friend.

"But I'd like to know why *he* keeps staring over here," Ted grunted in disgust while squinting guardedly at the table where his Ivy was seated. "Though he looks more like he's checking you out."

Hannah's hand stilled in its passage over her neck. *She knew!* No wonder she was having that strange sensation of pressure on her back. "Describe the man to me," she demanded in a strained voice.

"Him?" Ted asked indifferently. "Black hair, the usual features. Looks cocksure of himself." He paused for a moment before continuing forlornly. "I guess I don't blame Ivy for falling for him. He looks like he could buy and sell me."

"Tell me when they're looking somewhere else," she

ordered. Sensing by the lessening of the pressure that his attention was elsewhere, she turned casually and let her eyes drift over the table. She saw immediately that Ted's description of Ivy was true. Her light brown hair was styled to curl under and caress her cheeks. She was small and dainty in a demure white dress. Her long slender neck was arched as she looked up with overawed large brown eyes when Yale leaned over to speak to her.

She was a timid gazelle being mesmerized by the overpowering panther. Anger surfaced in an instant surge. What was it in him that he needed to stalk such tender morsels? Anyone could see that Ivy was unhappy and floundering out of her depth.

She'd like to shake some sense into the young woman's empty head. Didn't she know she'd already found the man who'd love and cosset her the way she obviously needed? Didn't that stupid female know a man of Yale's caliber would only scorch her and then toss her aside? Ted, she fumed to herself, deserved better treatment and understanding.

She permitted her gaze to slide to the tuxedo-clad man who was listening attentively to something the elderly couple at the table was saying. If Ted said Ivy's icy glance could kill, her virulent one should have scorched a hole through Yale's hide.

Irritated by the strong reaction he had triggered in her, she tore her gaze away and saw Ivy clutch her purse and leave the table. It was obvious where she was heading and, on impulse, Hannah did the same after murmuring an excuse to Ted.

They were alone in the small lounge lined with well-lit mirrors. Ivy had sunk into a wicker chair before one of them and Hannah selected the one next to her.

"That's a lovely dress," Hannah said casually as she drew lipgloss over her mouth. While Hannah's dress was also white, it would have looked sophomoric on her, but was perfect on the younger woman.

"Thank you. So is yours," Ivy replied grudgingly.

Her large brown eyes darted apprehensively over her, and to Hannah she looked even more like a frightened gazelle wondering when the predator was finally going to pounce. She could understand Ted's desire to protect. Had she been wrong, and was that all Yale felt toward her?

"I'm Hannah Blake," she said conversationally. "I'm with Ted Watson and he told me he knew you."

The fine-boned hand applying lipstick shook. "Yes, I saw you with him." She had meant it to be a cool dismissal, but she couldn't prevent her voice from wavering.

Hannah had never acted in the role of peacemaker before and wondered at herself for even attempting it. Ted's woebegone expression came to mind, and she decided to forge ahead before someone came into the ladies' room and this opportunity would be lost.

"I'm an old friend of his, and nothing more," she said reassuringly. Heavens, from Ivy's tone, she was likening her to Stella. "He told me you won't answer his calls and he's very hurt."

This time the brown eyes managed to contain frost. "And since you seem to know all about it, I assume he told you why!"

"Yes, that you saw him being attacked by Stella Moore," Hannah said more sharply than she'd intended. She was already sorry that she'd even started. "May I tell you something about that barracuda? She's a bitter and frustrated woman who thrives on causing trouble between people. She evidently saw that something was warm and nice between you two and decided to stir the pot. And you, like a fool, fell for it instead of trusting that sweet man who's so crazy over you that he can't see straight! It's time you grew up and saw people for what they are instead of reacting like a child to what is so obvious to everyone else!"

She had either killed or cured, she thought in exasperation as she left the lounge. She hadn't meant for her temper to erupt. The first course was on the table and she joined Ted in resolutely refraining to look at or mention anything more about the people at the table behind her.

Once again she admired the large ballroom with the handsome painted designs on the ceiling. The Breakers had been built in the era when elegance held importance and was in sharp contrast to the plastic functionalism of the newer hotels.

The obligatory speeches were given after dessert, thanking the patrons for participating in the one-hundred-dollar-a-plate charity ball. The orchestra then began playing and Ted asked hesitantly if she was up to dancing with him. He wasn't the worst dancer whom she'd partnered. At least his shuffling kept him from tramping on her feet.

"It's a slow one," she said, laughing. "I guess we can manage it."

Her antenna was at work. She saw Ivy and Yale immediately, the young woman's head barely reaching his shoulder as they moved over the dance floor. The first time they passed each other, she affected surprise at seeing Yale, and gave him a social smile. His knowing smile in return made her avert her eyes, but not before she'd caught the yearning look Ivy was giving Ted.

Her talk must have done some good, she thought virtuously. And she was certain it was that conviction that made her act the way she did a little later.

The dancers paused, waiting patiently for the orchestra to start a new selection. She had maneuvered Ted so they were next to Ivy and Yale. She smiled silkily at Yale as Ted stood stiffly by her side.

"Yale Upton, Ted Watson, an old friend of mine," she

said introducing the two men. They nodded perfunctorily, not shaking hands, she noticed. "It's good to see you again, Yale," she murmured over her thudding heart. "How about changing partners for this dance. Ivy and Ted are dear friends and I'm sure won't mind dancing together."

"Very brazen, hussy," he said into the hair tumbling over her ear as they moved off to the music. "Could you tell me what that was all about?"

Her smile showed her satisfaction. "It's very simple. They had a lovers' fallout and it was time something was done to bring them together."

They had a last look of Ted's dazed face and of the shy smile trembling on Ivy's lips before intervening couples hid them from view. "Besides," Hannah added firmly, "she's much too young for you!"

"Does that mean you find yourself more suitable?" Laughter rode his question and Hannah was suddenly embarrassed over her impetuous gesture. What must he be thinking of her? First, he'd had to put her to bed suffering from too much wine, and now she'd practically thrown herself at him, using the questionable excuse that she was trying to lure his partner for the evening into the arms of another man.

"I wasn't thinking about us," she said stiffly and, in that flash, she knew she was telling a lie. She saw with startling clarity that Ted's problem had been but the surface reason for acting so out of character. Ever since knowing Yale was in the same room, she'd yearned to be where she was now, in his arms.

"I'm not complaining," he said kindly. "I find dancing with you very pleasurable."

Oh, yes, she agreed heartily. It was very pleasurable indeed with her senses filled with the remembered scent of him and the warmth of his body under her hand resting on his shoulder.

To still her racing thoughts she said hurriedly, "Ted's an old friend and I acted on impulse when I saw a way to help him."

"Far be it from me to hinder love's tender blossoming." His cheek moved to where it rested against her temple and she knew he was smiling. Good Lord, when had they blended so close to each other? His arm tightened, stilling her involuntary move to pull away.

There was no struggle. She confessed to holding no desire to permit any space between them. By the time they circled the floor, her soft curves had instinctively found their proper resting place against the hard muscles of his body.

"I'm sorry," she murmured.

"Hmm?" he questioned into her hair.

"About the other night," she continued. "It must have been distasteful to you to see me in the state I was. I must have said some unforgivable things. You didn't call after that." Now what made her say that! He'd never mentioned anything about seeing her again.

"The reason you didn't hear from me is because I was out of town," he said, ending her flurry of self-denunciation. "I returned this afternoon and was going to call you, when I saw my secretary's note reminding me of this affair. Mr. Bryan, Ivy's father, is the man I'm buying out, and the invitation had been given several weeks ago."

"Oh!" Behind the sigh was the week of frustration and careful blocking of concern. That simple answer had never occurred to her.

He loosened his hold to look down at her, his gaze moving over the golden shoulders and lingering at the shadowy V between her breasts. "Have you had enough of this?" he asked. "I've had a tiring week and would just as soon get out of this crowd."

"But Ted . . ." she began.

"Leave that to me," he said, dancing her to the corner of the floor where Ted was swaying, his arms around a glowing Ivy, as if he'd never let her go.

He exchanged some words with Ted to which he nodded eagerly. Yale then released her to take Ivy's arm and lead her back to her parents' table.

"Come," Ted said hurriedly. "Get your purse and we'll split."

Hannah, assuming they were leaving to form a foursome someplace more quiet, left under his urging.

They waited outside the ballroom in the long hall lined with a floral runner while Yale and Ivy made their excuses to her parents.

Once outside, it seemed only natural that Ivy should slide into the HRG with Ted and she join Yale in his Porsche.

"Where are they going?" she asked in surprise on seeing the HRG turn in a different direction.

"I wouldn't know," Yale said. "Ted's a big boy and should know what he wants."

"And I suppose you do also." She had assumed incorrectly. There evidently had been no talk of remaining a foursome. She glanced at his profile to catch the reflection of strong white teeth flash in a very predatory smile.

"Very much so, my dear Ms. Hannah Blake," he said firmly. "Were you ever in doubt?"

A tingle of excitement danced down her spine. Anticipatory excitement, she admitted honestly. But something warned her not to permit the evening to end the way he was inferring. He already had too strong a hold on her emotions and he could hurt her too deeply in her vulnerable state.

"Thank you," she said sedately when he parked in front of her building. "You did say you'd had a busy week and were tired. Have a good rest."

His eyes glinted with mocking amusement when he unlatched his seat belt. "So prim and proper!" he goaded. "I expect at least a cup of coffee for rescuing you from that lovelorn Lothario."

Again he performed his magic, Hannah conceded with a shake of her head. She'd had no intention of inviting him into her apartment, and here she was in the kitchen filling the coffeepot with water while he was selecting mugs from the cupboard. How did he do it?

"Was your week successful?" she asked while removing a coffee cake from the freezer and placing it into the oven to heat.

"Enough," he said noncommittally. "What have you been doing besides acting as cupid to ex-boyfriends?"

She gave him a dazzling smile, recalling the happy faces on the two as they'd driven off. "That's one of my more successful ventures." She told him about Stella's act that had caused all the trouble. "You have no idea how his romances collapse in the most hilarious ways from his innocent bumbling." She laughed aloud, thinking of some of his past stories. "I hope Ted has the sense to nail Ivy down with a ring before he runs into another problem."

An eyebrow arched. "You believe a ring is necessary?" he mocked.

A cold finger touched her heart in warning. "Ivy is young enough to need that reassurance that he truly loves her," she said stiffly.

He nodded his head slightly in admission. "I've almost forgotten how they think when they are so immature. I've given an occasional ring, but I'd hate to think the women involved ever thought of them as anything but thanks for past favors."

That was putting all the cards on the table, Hannah admitted bitterly, concentrating on pouring the coffee without spilling a telltale drop, but what did she expect? Any man who reached his mid-thirties and was still a confirmed bachelor knew how to handle his love life without needing to give any commitments, especially a man as self-assured as he was.

She watched him add a drop of cream to his coffee while she sipped from her mug, aware of a sense of desolation, as if laying a dream to rest before she ever admitted to it. Yale wanted her, she knew, and she didn't know if she could, or even wanted to resist him. He was interested in only a limited affair. But she could have offered so much more!

CHAPTER FOUR

"I've contacted your office to tell them I'm looking for a manager," Yale informed her. "With the expansion of my company, I find I'm spreading myself too thin and I need someone to do the actual running of the production end."

"I'm certain Mr. Dunn will be able to locate someone you can work with," she said confidently, already mentally running through the file of potentials and wondering who Mr. Dunn would choose from the office to follow up on the request.

He rose to refill his mug and went to the living room. He discarded his jacket and loosened his tie before turning on the television to hear the late news.

Nothing like making himself at home, Hannah thought wryly as she followed him.

"Sit here," he ordered, patting the cushion next to him on the sofa.

No, her mind warned her even as she sank down beside him. He settled into the cushion before pulling her into the circle of his arm with her back against his chest and her head resting on his shoulder. They sat in comfortable silence as they sipped their coffee and watched the commentator expound on the day's news.

When the newscaster was through, Yale snapped off the set with the remote control and took her cup from her hand to place it on the side table with his.

"I hope you've noticed," he said with laughter moving along his suddenly sensuous mouth, "that I've been very careful not to ply you with wine tonight."

"But you don't know what I had at dinner," she said quickly, recalling with instant clarity his parting words before tucking her into bed the week before.

"You had exactly one glass of red wine," he reminded her, letting her know she'd been under constant surveillance, as she'd suspected. "And surely that should have no effect on you by now."

She was rotated in his arms as she spoke and her chin grasped so her face was raised for his inspection. "Cat's eyes," he murmured. "Beautiful amber cat's eyes that can flash with yellow fire when angry or, as now, become seductive bedroom eyes capable of driving a man to sell his soul."

His lips were light as he pressed her eyes closed. "And skin of pure silk," he continued, placing feathery kisses in a path down her smooth cheek to pause at the corner of her mouth already softening in expectation. "And lips dipped in honey; what promises do they hold?" He took a deep breath before fastening his mouth on hers in a search for the answer.

He's doing it again! Since being rocked by his kiss on his sailboat, Hannah had been wondering if it had been simply the romance of the setting that had sent her senses into orbit. There was no doubt now that it was Yale's expertise that had her responding thirstily, as if she'd been deprived too long of the nectar he provided. Her heart pounded heavily in her breast as her hands moved in restless exploration over the thin material of his shirt.

He probed along her lips with the tip of his tongue until her lips parted in eager compliance. She was pushed hard against the cushions as their tongues entwined in a sensuous mating dance for long, delirious minutes.

"Come," he whispered huskily, "not here." He drew her from the sofa. When they reached the bedroom door, cold reason intruded. Was this what she really wanted? she asked herself. The terrible letdown after her ex-fiancé's attempt at lovemaking had left her with a negative feeling about this type of commitment. True, Jim had never brought her to this fever pitch of aching yearning, but wasn't what happened in bed the same no matter with whom? Three times she'd tried it with him and had found the experience less than satisfying.

"No." She grasped the door jamb to halt their progress.

His arm tightened fractionally around her waist on seeing the strained expression on her face. "Hannah, look at me," he urged gently. "Trust me. It will be beautiful. But I promise we'll go no further than you want to."

His hand slid caressingly over her throat, moving slowly until the tension eased. Her body was telling her this was what it wanted. Perhaps this once she could tolerate the disappointing letdown that was bound to follow. The thought flitted briefly, to be lost in the web of the silvery haze he was weaving expertly over her senses as his mouth claimed hers.

"Take off my shirt," he whispered, releasing her when they stood by her bed. Trancelike, she obeyed, undoing the gold cufflinks on his sleeves with trembling fingers before slowly unbuttoning the pearl studs down his formal shirt. He stood silently, his gray eyes never leaving her face as she concentrated on her work. She'd seen him in swim trunks, but this sensuous disrobing was a new experience that was sending convolutions of heated awareness through her. Her hands moved lingeringly over the hair of his chest as they traveled upward to push the fine linen from his shoulders.

The snug trousers held the shirt in. No words were spoken, but under his compelling eyes she unfastened the belt buckle and opened the button beneath so the shirt could be removed.

He turned her around gently and worked the zipper down the back of her dress, helping her to step out of it before draping it carefully over a chair. Hannah was vibrantly aware of his eyes traveling over the lacy semi-bra and the long, lace-edged half slip when he turned back to her. They stood inches apart in their underclothes as his hands moved in slow exploration along her arms and across her throat before tracing the fullness of her breasts. His movements were unhurried; it was as if he were savoring the discovery of her every curve before the long tapered fingers found the front closing, sending the strapless bra to the carpet. His thumbs hooked over the half slip and panty hose, drawing them both off with practiced ease.

Her eyes were fastened on his face and she saw the sudden throbbing of the vein at his temple. A deep satisfaction touched her from the knowledge that she could stir this strong man so thoroughly. Her breasts were soon achingly swollen under his seductive stroking, and a heavy weight seemed to have settled in the pit of her body, causing her knees to feel alarmingly weak.

"Yale!" The moan held a plea that brought a small smile of acknowledgment to his lips.

"Touch me," he ordered huskily. "Do the same to me."

Her hands moved eagerly in their quest. His hard biceps twitched slightly in pleasure as her hands moved searchingly up his arms and across the wonderful width of his shoulders. Jim had been hairless, and she savored the new sensation of the curly hair as her hands continued their course through the mat covering Yale's chest. On encountering his nipples, an overwhelming impulse took over and she bent to flick her tongue over them. A tremor ran through him and her body vibrated with one of matching intensity. She breathed deeply of his male scent that seemed to increase with his arousal.

Her mouth lined a path of moist kisses to the warm curve of his neck. She was completely entranced by the mutual seduction they were performing. Her search continued over his rib cage, and relished the taut contraction of muscles over his flat stomach as her palm moved in slow circles as his had done minutes before on her. She then traced the hirsute outline over his chest and down his abdomen until she stopped at his briefs.

She hesitated, suddenly shy. "Yes," he answered her unasked question huskily. "Take them off. I want you to know me as I do you."

Her thumbs hooked over the elastic band and she tugged as he had done. She swayed, her breath catching in her throat. Her hands went to his hips to steady herself as she was swept into a whirlpool of emotions on being exposed to the evidence of his desire.

He pulled her close, his mouth on hers in flaming need. His hand searched and excited as he urged her to continue to follow his example. He was the teacher and she the avid pupil, both enthralled by the lessons being exchanged.

When he moved her to the bed she couldn't help the instinctive stiffening rejection. This wonderful foreplay was so much more than she'd ever expected, and she didn't want to ruin it by a repeat of the empty bewilderment she'd suffered through under Jim's self-serving exercise. Still, wasn't it up to her to give what he wanted in payment for introducing her to this exquisite excitement?

"What is it, Hannah?" he whispered, his gaze fastened

on her face. "Don't worry, I'll take care of everything so nothing will happen."

She looked at him, startled by what he was inferring. Becoming pregnant had never entered her mind. "I wasn't . . . I mean," she began helplessly.

His eyes narrowed, probing searchingly through her confusion. A hand cupped the side of her cheek while the thumb rubbed her lower lip, swollen from his kisses.

"Trust me, my sweet." He whispered the promise along the warm curve of her neck. "It will be good. You're a torch ready to be lit. Let me do it. Let me show you how wonderful it is to flame in complete surrender."

His mouth took over from his thumb, expertly removing all lingering hesitation. His roused body pressed against hers became the ultimate in exquisite rapture. There was no further room for introspection. Every intensely alive nerve was tuned to this moment and was quivering, ready for his torch.

"Yes, yes, please," she gasped, burning achingly for the culmination of his promise.

She was a musical instrument being tuned by a master's hand. When he pressed her to the bed, she waited in exultation for him to start the rhapsody that was crying for expression. It would be beautiful, she knew with throbbing certainty.

When his muscular thigh finally parted hers, and they soared on the full power of their passion, the music that thundered in her ears was more exquisite than any she'd ever dreamed possible. When the last note faded, she felt replete in spite of a new yet wonderful exhaustion.

"I didn't know," she whispered into the moist warmth of his chest. "Is this what I've been missing?"

His arms moved convulsively, binding her to him. "Now you know," he growled. "But let me warn you, woman, you've got my brand on you now and you'd better not experiment with anyone else!"

She raised her lashes to look at him, ready to laugh at what she was certain he intended as a joke. She was momentarily taken aback by the fierce expression on his face.

"I've never been the promiscuous type," she said with forced lightness, wondering if he felt the responding increase in tempo of her heart at his words. Was he thinking in terms of an affair? And when it was over, would he give her a ring as a parting gift for favors once shared? The pain that shot through her was so intense that her body flinched.

He misinterpreted the movement. "I'm sorry, I'm too heavy on you," he apologized, rolling to his side before molding her to him.

With the warm strength of him beside her, her body was too happy to permit the bleak thought to return. She could see how easy it would be to slide into an affair with him. Sleeping with him could be very addictive. He'd taken her to heaven and plucked a handful of stars, dazzling her with their brilliance before offering them as a present and she was already longing for an armful.

She woke up, clutching at him when he went to move from his side. "Where are you going?" she asked sleepily, already missing the warm contact.

"It's late, or early, depending on how you look at it," he answered. "I don't care to return home in the daylight still in my tuxedo." His mouth touched her cheek and she quickly wrapped her arms about him.

"Don't leave me," she whispered, tracing kisses along the curve of his neck. "Don't go now. Stay just a little longer." She was begging, something she never thought she'd be capable of doing. Her body pressed instinctively against his while her hands wound in his hair.

His response was instantaneous. "No, not now," he agreed, his mouth, his body telling of his own aroused desire.

Once again he transported her to where the driving need of their bodies drove all coherent thoughts from her mind and on into the ecstasy of their fusion.

"Thank you," she murmured when she was able to talk once more.

He was leaning partially over her, his hands lazily fanning her silken hair over the pillow. He paused in his stroking, his chest moving against her breasts as he chuckled. "What a crazy thing to say," he answered, "but nice to hear. May I say I found it very enjoyable also?" His tongue traced the full curve of her lower lip. "In fact it was downright fantastic," he amended before taking ownership of her mouth in a final kiss before he levered himself from her.

"Don't move," he ordered quickly when she started to reach for him. "I want to hold this picture of you. A bewitching woman, surfeited by love. My love."

Her body arched slightly toward him as his gaze traveled from her tousled hair and face slackened by passion spent to the rosily flushed and damp body that had known his complete possession. She had been touched by those gray eyes already but there was a new light in them, as if flames that before had remained camouflaged by the smoke had finally broken through.

"Sleep, sweet heart," he said when, after dressing, he pulled a sheet over her and bent to kiss her. "I'll call later this afternoon."

She nodded drowsily, loving the way he broke the commonplace "sweetheart" into two words, giving them special meaning. She was fast asleep before the lock clicked behind him on leaving the apartment.

Hannah drifted awake when the morning was half gone.

What a beautiful, glorious day, she breathed, hugging herself with happy wonder as she gazed out of the window at the overcast sky.

She drank her orange juice and coffee, staring dreamily at nothing in particular, a bemused expression on her face. Not until she recalled his parting words that he'd call in the afternoon did her languorous mood dissipate.

While showering, the soaped washcloth sliding over her body reawakened the paths long tapered hands had traveled with tingling knowledge. She hurriedly rinsed and left the steamy cubicle to dry herself briskly, using one stimulus to eradicate another more sensual one.

By two o'clock she was sitting tensely by the phone, willing it to ring while trying not to torture herself over doubts that his promise held no substance and was nothing more than a lightly given farewell. What, after all, did she really know about this man who had stormed and so easily breached her citadel? What did she know except his kiss rendered her incapable of thought and the promise of his caressing hands had her melding against him in quivering acquiescence?

She was pacing the floor as the clock neared six. By that time Hannah's emotions had run the full gamut from fervid anticipation to bleak acceptance that she'd been alone in her transport the night before. She'd given of herself as never before and had thought Yale had done the same. Had his response tricked her into building impossible dreams on false assumptions?

Did he transport all his women the same way? Lucky, lucky women, and what a fool she was! She should have remembered her evaluation on their initial meeting. A dangerous man, her instinct had warned her. If she'd avoided him as had been her first inclination, she'd still be safely wrapped within her unawakened emotions and not torn apart.

She'd been content with the string of dates, accepting the tepid warmth of their kisses simply because she hadn't known the flames one man's lips could evoke.

When the phone rang shortly after six, her pique had reached a high that almost caused her to ignore it. Almost.

"Hannah," he said in a deep purr, and with that one word all conflicting turmoil was laid to rest.

"Hello, Yale," she answered softly, surprising herself by feeling suddenly shy. Last night she'd slept with the man, for gosh sakes! There'd been no part of each other that they hadn't explored in fervent rhapsody.

"I'm sorry I'm so late getting to you, but I slept late." His voice took on a deeper vibrancy. "It seems I ran into this Venus last night and she gave me this cup of coffee that had some aphrodisiac in it."

"You have to be careful of people like that," Hannah admonished, muffling the laughter. She was suddenly wonderfully, ecstatically happy. "Even as a child, my father always warned me not to take anything from strangers."

"Mmm. Yes, so was I, but, you see, she was so enticing, I was certain one so bewitching would never stoop to anything so underhanded."

"I see you have a problem. Perhaps you'd better stay away from her." What was she saying!

"I've a better plan," he answered. "You see, I'm in a quandary. I don't know if it's that coffee she fed me or something more lethal. I've been accused of being very tenacious when solving a problem. Do you think you can be ready in thirty minutes? I need you to help me unravel the reason for such irrational behavior."

"Irrational?" she repeated in a small shocked voice.

"Completely, exhilaratingly, gloriously irrational!" he returned in a deep growl that made her heart jerk with memories of how his chest had vibrated against her breasts when he used that tone the night before. "I slept the afternoon away and now I have a terrible need to see if you're real. Will you be ready in half an hour?"

"Yes," she answered breathlessly. Thirty minutes, ten minutes, *now*. Only hurry!"

"Good. I know this little out-of-the-way Italian restaurant." He paused, then asked, as if it were important, "You do like Italian food?"

"With a passion," she admitted.

"Somehow I knew you did," he said with a chuckle. "See you."

Hannah stared happily into space before she pulled herself together with a jerk. Here she was wasting precious minutes daydreaming when she should be dressing!

She was blotting her lipstick with a tissue when the knock came on the door, alerting her of his arrival. She quickly applied a spray of her favorite perfume. A glance at her wristwatch showed he was a man of his word. Thirty minutes to the second. She tucked that information away for future reference.

She flung the door open, a happy anticipatory smile wreathing her face. He stood tall and imposing in hiphugging jeans and a black polo shirt. His fists were braced on his hips; an angry frown closed the space between his dark brows.

Her smile faltered on seeing his threatening stance. "Yale?" The timid word showed her bewilderment.

"Do you always open your door like that without first checking to see who's there?" he snapped. "Don't you have any sense at all?"

With her known temper, her reaction was predictable. In the business world she had found that the best defense is an offense. Yellow lights flared from amber eyes. "Only neighbors knock on apartment doors. *Guests* are supposed to ring for admittance at the front door. How did you manage to sneak your way in?" The words were enunciated clearly so that there'd be no doubt in his mind about the anger seething behind them. How dare he accost her that way!

His black lashes lowered, shadowing his eyes as he evaluated with cool detachment the flush anger brought to her face. "One of your neighbors was leaving and let me in. Perhaps you all need a lesson on security. Also a course on commonsense protection, in which you all seem to be sadly lacking."

His condescending tone sent her temper up a notch. "Common sense!" Her voice vibrated with anger. She took a deep breath in an obvious struggle for control. Her lips parted in an icy smile. "I dare say you're right about security, Mr. Upton," she murmured in a saccharine voice, "and there's no better time than the present to start practicing it."

The door was slammed shut on his face before he could stop her. She let him hear the grate of the lock and the noise of the chain restraint as she slipped it in place. He preached security, did he? She'd show him!

She waited tensely for his knock as new words sprang to mind with which to castigate him. It took several minutes before she realized there wasn't going to be one. The soft whirr of the elevator down the hall warned her that he was leaving.

All anger drained from her as she sagged weakly against the door. What had she done? she cried in horror. There'd been no cause for her to flare into such a violent reaction. He'd been right. The papers warned daily about such carelessness as she'd just exhibited. A laugh, a welcoming kiss would have smoothed his irritation. Instead, she'd sent him away and she was dazed by the shattering force of his rejection. The intercom to the front door buzzed and she flew to answer it, her body trembling with the surge of hope.

The speaker made all voices sound tinny, but there was no doubt whose it was. "Yale Upton here."

An exultation hit her. He hadn't left after all! Her finger shook as she pressed the release button and she waited impatiently by the door for his knock.

"Who is it?" she asked coolly when it came.

"The big bad wolf," he growled, and she laughed as she hurriedly undid the lock.

This time she made certain she obeyed his orders. She peered through the crack caused by the restraining chain. "Why, hello, Mr. Wolf," she said demurely before releasing the chain. "Won't you come in?"

He was in the room, closing the door behind him with his foot and sweeping her into his arms before she could step back. She met his kiss with a hunger that equaled his. The last one shared had been all too long ago and she felt as if she had been on a starvation diet.

"That's better," he said huskily against her lips. "I don't know what got into us before. Something just flared up in me over how you were permitting yourself to be exposed to possible trouble."

Hannah's lashes fluttered demurely as she drew a finger along the firm outline of his jaw. She couldn't deny the pleasure coursing through her over his desire to protect. It was a warming sensation.

"You did come on heavy," she agreed. "Let me warn you that I've always had a short fuse whenever someone attempts to order me around."

He caught the trailing finger and nibbled on its soft pad. "Lesson taken. Will it do if I preface future orders with a *please?*" His eyes were laughing down at her, but somehow they warned her not to take what had happened lightly.

She swayed to him, her knees rubbery from the spiraling sensations started by his light nipping. Even that small act created heat waves to course through her. Already she was losing control over her usually obedient emotions. Oh, yes, he was a very dangerous man. But even if he had been painted with a warning skull and crossbones, she knew she had passed beyond any restraining caution. After the night they had just shared, every last inch of her body was quivering with a longing to be back in his arms. And tonight, after their dinner . . .

"You'd better stop looking at me like that or we'll never get beyond that door," Yale growled in warning. "You're presenting a problem, woman. I'm caught between two hungers, but since I haven't had anything beyond a snack this morning, I think I'd better take care of that appetite first, so I can do justice to the other one later."

His fingers dug into her shoulders while he gave her a swift, hard kiss. He then moved her away from him and watched with sympathetic understanding as her hands fumbled with the strap of her pocketbook that she hung over her shoulder. Unfortunately she didn't suffer from his indecision. She knew which hunger she'd prefer satisfying first.

The decor at Pasquale's was overdone with raffia-wrapped wine bottles everywhere and canned Italian music, but the food was delicious. The antipasto was cold and tasty, the chicken Tetrazzini superb, and the carafe of red wine perfect. The owner, his liquid brown eyes telling of his Latin origin, informed them that the wine was imported from the vineyards of his hometown. "Nothing but the best for my customers," he said, his white teeth flashing, acknowledging their approval.

Yale, Hannah noticed with hidden amusement, limited her intake to two glasses. There would be no repeat of the ignominious end to the dinner they'd shared in her apartment!

"How soon will you be needing the new supervisor for your plant?" Hannah asked. They were sipping aromatic espresso after refusing dessert. Their conversation had ranged over many topics, mostly impersonal, as if recognizing the need to temporarily defuse the heated current that flowed between them.

"As soon as we sign the final papers and the building's mine. Your father said it should be in two weeks. There are still some minor details that need ironing out. Luckily the building was used mainly as a warehouse and we will be putting only a few people out of work. I already offered jobs to them if they want to be retrained."

He'd have that concern, Hannah realized. He was a strong-willed person, but this touch of compassion was part of his character. He'd be an easy person to fall in love with, she reflected, and pulled herself short at the thought. Love? She skimmed around the circumference of the idea, testing it cautiously. Would she dare let that happen? After what was shared the night before, she could consider an affair with him. Consider was the wrong word, she admitted. She was already launched into one. She enjoyed her work and the independence it gave her, and at twenty-seven she had built a satisfying life-style that she had no intention of changing. From the evidence around her, and after her disastrous engagement, she had no desire to try the marriage route, at least not at present. An affair she could handle. It would be less painful to end. Divorces were messy at best.

Besides, love was not necessary in such an alliance. Respect, yes. And admiration. She had both for the dynamic man sitting across from her. And it was undeniable he held the key, that to date no other man had possessed, to bringing her emotions into high eruption. The immediate future was rosy indeed.

Yale placed his elbows on the table as he leaned toward her. "You know, you have the most remarkable eyes, Hannah," he mused, his voice the deep purr that never failed to stir her. "I've never seen that particular amber color. Yet, when you're angry, yellow sparks shoot from them and, at times, like now, they're dark honey, all melting and enticing bedroom eyes. What are you thinking about, sweet heart?" Again he separated the word, giving it an added endearment that thrilled. "I know what I'm thinking about, and I'm calling for the check."

He leaned back and signaled to the waiter. He finished the wine in his glass, letting his gaze ride over her. A satisfied smile touched his mouth on seeing her soft lips part as if in anticipation.

He barely scanned the check when presented before placing a bill on it. "Come," he said, not hiding his urgency. "Let's get out of this place."

They skirted the closely packed tables when a hand reached out to stop Yale. "Darling," the dark-haired woman cried. "Fancy meeting you here! Isn't this a little out of your territory?"

She was smoothly attractive with a carefully cultivated tan that Hannah instinctively knew stopped at no white patches on her body. She'd be golden from head to toe.

"No more than you are, Theda. I hope you'll enjoy the meal as much as we have." Yale made a move to leave, but the beautifully manicured hand remained on his arm.

"Oh, we're finished. Won't you join us in an after-dinner drink?" Her eyes were noncommittal in their evaluation as they swept over Hannah. "I'd like you to meet my friends." She introduced her escort and the other couple with her and Yale performed the duty with Hannah.

Theda's hand had slipped down into his and was clasping it tightly. "Do stop for a drink, darling, for old times' sake," she said huskily, her smile telling him of remembered secrets. "I thought I saw you this afternoon on Worth Avenue, then was certain when you took off in your Porsche. Who was the gorgeous blonde with you? Still playing the field, I see." Her gaze slid obliquely to see how Hannah took that bit of information.

Hannah's smile froze. With painful clarity, she recalled Yale's assertion only short hours before. *I slept the afternoon away,* he'd said, and in her bemused state she'd believed him, fool that she was. Had he sweet-talked the blonde into believing a similar story in dropping her for the night? A more horrendous thought hit her. Had he discovered the blonde was unable to go out with him this evening and that was the reason why he'd called her so late for this date?

Yale glanced at her to see if she wished to join them. His eyes narrowed on seeing the set look to her face and he gave his apologies before leading her out.

He let the strained silence continue until they were halfway to her apartment. "What gives, Hannah?" he asked with a sigh. "Something's bothering you and you might as well get it off your chest."

"Nothing's bothering me," she said with false sweetness. "But I do think it's amazing that you still have all five fingers on your hand."

He shot her a startled look before a smile of understanding deepened the crease lining his cheek. "Are you referring to Theda? Shame on you! I thought you too smart to be taken by her tactics." He maneuvered a turn before he shot her another glance. "Could it be that there's a little green lurking in those remarkable eyes of yours?"

Hannah stared stonily ahead, aware of the male pleasure he was deriving at the thought. Jealousy had nothing to do with what she was feeling, she swore. She'd given him time to explain why he had lied to her about his afternoon, but he evidently didn't think it was any of her business. It wasn't, she admitted, and that was what hurt. But she was a very fastidious person. If he wished to continue to play the field, there was no way she could stop him, but she wouldn't be one of his incidental pastimes. He'd have to decide that if he wanted her, he'd have to be faithful as long as their liaison was in effect.

While Jim meant nothing to her anymore, it still pained to remember that he had been sleeping around while they were engaged. At the time she swore she'd never expose herself to such a degrading humiliation again. She'd just been given a warning and this time she was smart enough to heed it before becoming further involved.

"Thanks for the dinner," she began when he pulled into the parking lot serving her apartment.

His mouth firmed in anger at her obvious intention to end the evening there. He slammed out of the car and her door was jerked open before she could say more. His hand hooked under her arm and she was pulled out and marched to the entrance. He waited in cold silence while she selected the key to open the door.

If he thought he was getting an invitation inside, he had another thought coming, she fumed, incensed by his overbearing tactics. "I said, thank you for the dinner," she began again, only to be marched to the elevator. Unfortunately it opened at once to the touch of the button and she was hustled inside.

"Listen to me," she stormed as the elevator rose. "I'm not in the mood to entertain tonight. I'm a working girl and I have an early appointment in the morning. I'm tired and intend to go to bed early."

He looked purposefully at his wristwatch. "At eight thirty?" he asked caustically.

She bit her lip in vexation. "I find I'm not quite over the effects of the flu," she prevaricated quickly.

"I shall be gone by ten," he said, leading her to her door.

If he got inside, she knew he'd only have to take her in his arms and she'd be lost, leaving her to hate herself once he was gone. Somehow she'd have to make him understand she had no intention of letting that happen. In the past she'd managed other persistent dates without too much trouble and she quickly weighed her options as she inserted the key.

She had defused many amorous hopefuls with humorous but pointed quips, but she knew instinctively that wouldn't faze the determined man beside her, neither would cold disdain. He'd hustle her inside before she could send in the barb, as he had done in the elevator. Her only recourse was to tell him what he had asked for in the beginning—what actually was bothering her, what had turned the heated current that had flowed between them into a refrigerant.

She turned to him, her stare frosted. "Tell me, Yale, how did you manage to get in a date with that blonde Theda mentioned and also sleep away the afternoon as you informed me? What was the need to tell me the lie?"

She felt rather than saw the jerk that hit him. His eyes matched hers in their icy overlay. The elevator door opened and a neighbor, after a quick glance at them, stepped hurriedly out of their way.

Yale glanced over his shoulder at the man and it was all the distraction she needed. She was inside her apartment with the locks quickly thrown before he could move. She leaned against the door, breathing hard as if she'd just run a marathon. Her eyes closed as she drew a long, shuddering breath. She had succeeded, but the escaping whimper indicated the intensity of the pain stabbing in her chest.

The door vibrated under his heavy pounding. "Hannah, open up," he called menancingly.

She covered her ears, but the noise continued, forcing her to answer. "Go away," she hissed. "I have nothing more to say to you."

"You'd better open up and now," he warned. "I won't stop until you let me in."

"Go away. You'll upset all the neighbors," she wailed.

A few choice words were thankfully muffled by the door. "Hannah!" he roared. "I'm warning you! I'm not leaving!"

And he wouldn't either, she knew. The neighbors' heads would soon be out their doors. Reluctantly she drew the bolt and stepped back hastily as he came storming in. She was immediately aware she'd made a terrible mistake. His face was white with rage. She'd never seen a man so fulminatingly angry.

CHAPTER FIVE

"No one has ever shut a door in my face before," he enunciated coldly as he moved threateningly toward her. "And you've done it twice in one day. You, my dear, have one big lesson to learn."

His intention was all too clear. Hannah put out a protesting hand in a hopeful attempt to stop his intimidating approach. She hastily back-stepped when she saw that gesture was futile, until her retreat was stopped by the sofa pressing into the calves of her legs.

"Yale, please!" she entreated. "We're grown people. You can't do this to me!"

"No?" he growled. This time there was no purr in his voice. He moved incredibly fast. He grabbed her shoulders, his fingers curling into the softness of her skin with angry intensity.

She winced from the pain. And in her fury, she raised her hands to push him away.

As abruptly as she had been restrained, she was released from his searing grip. She swayed dizzily from the sudden movement and angrily watched him as he calmly stood before her with his hands on his hips.

"You have just had another lesson, young lady. Let me tell you, I never lie, and you'd better learn right now to trust me in that. Do you understand?"

Hannah didn't answer. She was too shaken and infuriated by what had just happened to utter coherent words.

"And now, since you claim you're so tired, I'll leave," he said tightly.

He strode to the door to pause with his hand on the knob as he glared back at her, showing his anger was only slightly abated. "I believe any relationship that doesn't contain mutual trust isn't worth keeping, Hannah. Do I make myself clear?" His eyes burned their message into her.

He left, closing the door with a quiet finality that spoke louder than had it been slammed.

Hannah stood for long seconds, staring blankly at the door while conflicting emotions tore through her. Trust. He'd kept repeating that word as though it were very important to him. Had doubting him been what had incensed him to react so forcefully?

She'd never been treated so summarily. No other man would ever have dared to. But then Yale was different from all the rest and she'd be wise to remember that. The chagrin over his harshness abated as she concentrated on his last pronouncement.

She had a good business head, calm and analytical. She had to, dealing with high-powered executives who often acted like prima donnas, and she brought it to use to find where she had possibly gone wrong.

It had been an evening that she'd long remember, starting as it had with her quixotic reaction to his proprietary words that caused her to lock him out the first time.

Proprietary? The word stuck in her mind, causing her

to pause. Before, she would have described his action as unnecessarily protective, but now with this deeper probing, his demand that she practice better security had a definite possessive ring.

A frown of annoyance appeared. She was too independent to tolerate anyone acting possessive about her. Her father, who had the greatest right, had made no objection when she'd taken an apartment. He recognized her need to be self-sufficient, to make her own decisions; in fact he was proud of the strides she was making on her own.

Did Yale think one shared night entitled him special privileges? How like a man, she fumed. With the return of her anger, she reviewed the disastrous end to the evening. He thought he was free to give her ultimatums, did he? Well, she had a few of her own. Like lies about dates with blondes, and a rapacious, sloe-eyed female who was assured enough to let his present date see she still staked a claim on him. She was no better than Stella Moore, whose advances had almost wrecked what had started between Ivy and Ted.

It was lucky she'd gone to that dance or Stella's dirty work would have won out. A faint smile touched her lips on recalling how successful her initial attempt at matchmaking had been. The happy faces of the two were worth the embarrassment she had at first felt when telling Ivy a few home truths about designing women and trust. *Trust!*

Her face paled as a new thought intruded. The parallel between Stella's action and Theda's were too close to be ignored. Had she walked into the same trap that Ivy had? She groaned as she struggled to recall Theda's exact words. *I thought I'd seen you,* the woman had said to Yale, and immediately she'd accepted it as the truth. But Yale hadn't refuted her words, she thought in some confusion, then admitted that if in his place, and confident under the wonderful vibes that had been flowing between them, she'd have assumed that he would recognize the lie. *Oh, Yale, what have I done!* No wonder he'd been so angry. Guilt and a nameless emotion filled her. A glance at her watch showed it was near ten. His house, she knew, wasn't far from hers and he should be home by now.

Without thinking further, she crossed to the phone and pulled out the directory. Hurriedly, before second thoughts stopped her, she dialed his number.

He answered on the second ring. "Upton here."

"Yale," she began, and swallowed hard to stop the quiver in her voice. What in the world was she doing? she wondered in panic.

"Hannah?"

The question showed his surprise and the envisioned confusion on his face caused her to relax slightly. "I'm calling to say I'm sorry. I've never reacted this way before. You were right, I deserved to be chastised for being discourteous to you." She was uptight again and she paused, hoping he'd say something to ease the situation. Had she been a fool to call?

"And what brought about this enlightenment?" he asked. His voice showed only idle interest, making Hannah decide she was indeed a fool. Why should he care? He evidently still nursed his anger.

She was aware of a dull hopeless feeling growing in her and a startling urge to cry. She'd better bring the senseless call to an end. "You were right about trust. I realized there wasn't much difference between Theda and Stella Moore."

"Stella?" he asked, momentarily unable to make the connection. "Ah, yes. The snake in Ivy and Ted's Eden."

Hannah drew a sigh of relief. He understood! "Good night, Yale," she said in a low voice. "I'm sorry if I disturbed you."

She hung up then. She might not have accomplished

anything, but giving the apology had helped lessen some inner tension, and hopefully she'd be able to get some sleep.

After tucking her hair in a protective cap, she adjusted the showerhead to needle spray and stepped under its force. She let the fine drill of hot water work its therapeutic benefit over her back. She'd found it relaxing in the past, and sleep was what she needed now more than anything. Tomorrow she'd face what, if anything, she could do about mending the rents in her relationship with Yale.

She rubbed herself dry before smoothing a favorite lotion over her body. Acquiring a tan was fine, but it did tend to dry the skin. She frowned on hearing a thudding noise and gave a groan. Fay, a recently divorced woman who lived across the hall, had the unhappy ability to frequently lock herself out of her apartment. Her keys for some reason were always misplaced. Freud would have had a field day unraveling the devious paths of her subconscious, she was sure.

After waking the disgruntled superintendent several times, she'd inveigled Hannah to hold a set for such emergencies. She now grabbed a robe out of her closet and slipped the key from the holder inside the kitchen door and hurried to unlock the door.

"Lost it again?" she asked with a sigh as she held the key out. Her hand dropped as did her mouth. Yale stood there tall and impossibly, overwhelmingly male in jeans and a checked cotton shirt, the upper buttons open, exposing dark curls of hair.

"It seems we've gone through this act before," he said tersely as he stepped into the room and turned the lock after closing the door with that silent force that sounded so alarmingly threatening.

"What . . . I mean, how?" She was too astounded to do more than stammer.

"Yes, I rang your bell and when you didn't answer, I assumed you must have turned it off," he explained, answering the question she was too stunned to utter. "Again there was an obliging tenant who let me enter with her." His chest moved with a sigh of resignation over the gullibility of people. "But that doesn't excuse you from not checking first before opening the door. Or do you hand out your key to anyone who comes this late at night?"

Hannah's skin prickled in apprehension at the threatening anger behind the cold smile, giving his face a forbidding look. Violence was there, held under tight control. "Am I, after all, one of many?"

Her reaction was instant. "How dare you!" she raged. "I thought you were my neighbor . . ." Her lips clamped tight. No! She wouldn't give him the satisfaction of an explanation. Damn him anyway! He had no right accusing her. "You're a fine one, mouthing words about trust," she stormed. "Get out of here, I never want to see you again!"

His fierce expression faded and Hannah found herself breathing a sigh of relief. For a moment she had been actually frightened.

A large hand kneaded the muscles of his neck. "We're doing it again," he said, a wry smile easing the tense lines from his face. "What is it that makes us spark off like this?"

"You had no right accusing me without cause," she said stiffly.

"Neither one of us has," he agreed philosophically. "But somehow I don't think that will stop us from flaring up again. You're a very challenging lady and you've been throwing me curves that keep catching me off-guard. Shall we make a pact to count to ten before letting it get out of hand again?" His smile now held the relaxed charm that had entrapped her before and she found herself responding all too readily.

"Well, trust has to work both ways," she countered smartly. "You were very specific in bringing home that little detail."

His fingers again kneaded the back of his neck in a gesture she was recognizing as one he performed when perturbed. He was before her, his hands moving slowly along the length of her upper arms. "What am I going to do about you, Hannah?" His voice was the low velvet rasp that sent thrilling ripples along her nerves. "You're slowly tying me into knots and I don't know if I should run scared or stay and wait it out." The fires in the back of his eyes told what he wished to do, and she met his gaze with the same intensity.

"Ah, sweet heart," he murmured, "I'm afraid the decision has been made for me. Who am I to fight my fate, especially when it's wrapped in such a seductive package?"

His eyes slid over her and only then did Hannah realize the robe she'd grabbed when going to answer the door was her pale blue satin one, trimmed with wide bands of ecru lace. She couldn't have chosen a more seductive covering, and she was fiercely glad. She wanted to appear perfect to this exciting man who could do such thrilling things to her nerves.

"When you called, I knew I had to come, that you wouldn't have done it if you didn't want me here. Besides, I was in no mood for a cold shower."

Was that really why she had called and not waited for the morning? She gave a happy sigh as his lips claimed hers. In the future she'd be wise to obey her instincts if they brought about this happy result.

It was a new kiss. Gentle and delightful behind its firmness. The thought startled her for a moment, to be swept away as his lips moved in a deeper probing. They searched in a hungry quest, as if needing assurance that he was in possession of her deepest commitment.

Her lips parted to give him that assurance, her tongue curling and meeting his until he retreated to let her discover the same delight in his mouth.

Their hands moved in an equal duet of discovery. Her satin robe rustled to the floor and they both worked feverishly to remove his clothes.

For silent moments he held her fiercely to him, his face buried in her hair with hers in his neck. Both breathed deeply, intoxicated by the other's unique body scent, warm and perfumed.

Pressed close to his side, they moved to the bedroom, both eager to ride the ever new excitement holding them in its grip. He held her away from him with a light clasp when they reached the bed. His gaze slid in burning examination of her slender body, pausing in delight over her already pointing breasts, moving enticingly under her rapid breathing, and on over her flat abdomen and to the promise shielded by the golden shadow at her thighs.

"You're exquisite," he murmured reverently, and watched as she performed the same exploration. Her amber eyes paused at the strong thrust of his neck and touched at the breadth of his shoulders. The hair covering his chest came next, and as if trapped by a magnet, she followed its path as it narrowed over his abdomen and spread again into a frame for his full arousal.

He saw the quick intake of breath and she was crushed to him, his mouth placing hot moist kisses on her face as he lowered her onto the bed.

Hannah was swept in a delirium of delight. How had she ever existed before? she wondered in quickening exultation. Whatever she'd felt for her fiancé had been a paltry exercise in search of an emotional high, she now knew as

Yale led her in an overwhelming exploration until no part of them were strangers to their hands, their mouths.

Several times, with devilish enticement when she was almost beyond reason and begging for his ultimate possession, he'd slowed the pace until their heartbeats could again be counted. When he finally rose over her and took her, she was caught up in total abandon, writhing, burying her nails in his flesh until he carried her over the threshold, almost senseless from the power of the explosions, and down the long slide back to reality, held safe in the cradle of his arms.

She gave a deep sigh and raised heavy lids to find him examining her face with curiously bright eyes. She hesitated, wondering with sudden embarrassment what he was thinking of her wanton behavior. Had those sounds really come from her throat? Had she actually arched herself into his thrust in that wild manner, urging him on with her hands gripping his buttocks?

"Ah, yes, you are indeed a Venus," he murmured gruffly. "But at this point I agree that what we both need is that sleep you so pointedly informed me that you wanted."

Hannah curled against the warmth of his body, letting her fingers quench their thirst for one last pleasurable dip through the curly hairs on his chest. A question had been nagging her and she shifted her head to take in the shadowed outline of his face against the pillow. "Trust means a lot to you, doesn't it?" she asked musingly. He'd mentioned it often enough to bring home that fact.

He stiffened slightly and his hand went over hers to still its movement. "I guess it does," he admitted slowly in a surprisingly strained voice. And there in the darkness he told of a wife and mother who loved too well but not wisely, who made his father's life miserable with her unreasonable jealousy, and his also with nagging insistence to pry into every facet of her son's life. "I saw what she was doing to my father and how we both were forced to build protective shields to hide behind so we could call our souls our own," he ended harshly. "It made me appreciate the value of trust. Perhaps at times I'm paranoid about it, but I made a vow early in life that no relationship was worth having unless it also held that vital ingredient."

He shifted to gather her close. "Enough of past ghosts. I've a more interesting present to take care of." His kiss placed a firm ending to his confession and effectively wiped it from her mind under the welling of the delicious sensations he so expertly aroused.

"Is this how you plan for us to catch up on our sleep?" she teased.

A chuckle, telling of his satisfaction with her response, rumbled in his chest. He released his hold but kept her in the haven of his arms. The last thing Hannah remembered was the deep contentment that filled her. She had found her reason for being. And he was beside her.

CHAPTER SIX

"You aren't listening," John said with irritation. "Brother, that must have been some weekend!"

"What?" Hannah asked, turning dream-filled eyes to her coworker. She shouldn't have come in, she admitted. She was finding it too difficult to dissimulate.

Sometime during the night Yale had kissed her awake and they'd shared another mind-bending experience in each other's arms. When the alarm had gone off, he was gone, but now all her body wanted was to remember each exquisite awakening he'd performed on it.

"Oh, never mind," John said gruffly. "But you'd better act more alert when in Dunn's office."

"Dunn's office?" she asked blankly.

John groaned. "That's what I've been telling you. I just left the big boss and he said he wants to see you in half an hour."

Her dreams scattered and with a frown she considered the files on her desk. Was there a question about someone in her caseload? Shortly before she'd been sick, he'd complimented her on her meticulous attention to details that had helped impress a client to hire one of their men. But then she hadn't as yet met a dangerously exciting man who absorbed all too much of her thoughts and wreaked havoc on her ability to concentrate.

Before complying, Hannah went to the washroom to check her makeup and see that her chignon was in its usual neat coil. She preferred skirts with the tailored blazers she wore to work. She never felt the need to either add to or detract from her femininity.

True, there were occasionally times when, like John's unexpected kiss, she was annoyed by attempts at the barriers she kept in place at work. Her strict attention to business usually kept sexual overtures under control. John had acted rashly under the influence of too many martinis at lunch. Not too strangely, he'd accepted her sharp setdown philosophically. There were enough pressures in their work without unsettling undercurrents interfering with their jobs.

The bass "Come in" answered her knock. The deep voice suited the head of Executives, Incorporated. He was only an inch taller than Hannah, but massive, not in soft fat, but in hard muscle. He was always immaculate, with hair streaked gray, barber fresh, and superbly tailored suits. His features were unremarkable, his expression bland. On first meeting one was likely to underrate him until one became conscious of how the piercing blue eyes were constantly evaluating, sorting, and filing. Hannah had come to regard his prodigious memory with awe.

"Sit down, Hannah," he ordered, his glance taking instant inventory of her smartly tailored outfit. Years from now, she was certain, he'd be able to describe it in minute detail.

He pulled a file from the bin on the corner of his desk and handed it to her. "This request came in Friday and I'm placing you on it. You did the Orlando Electronics job and this appears to be along the same line. You should be able to pull some possibilities left over from the contacts you made for them, since the requirements are almost identical."

Hannah read the neatly typed heading and wondered why she felt no surprise. Upton Enterprises. Somehow it seemed foreordained that she should be handling Yale's case.

"I think I should tell you first that my father's office is handling Mr. Upton's merger," she said hurriedly. She longed to handle the case. It would give her extra opportunities to communicate with Yale, but she couldn't if Mr. Dunn thought there'd be any conflict of interest.

Her expression was carefully controlled as he studied her while ingesting that bit of information. "I've never had to question your integrity," he said finally, and her long sigh alerted her to how she'd been holding her breath.

He quickly outlined what type executive supervisor was needed. It was much as she'd gleaned from Yale's conversation. "If his qualifications warrant it, he could be considered for a vice-presidency, but only hint at that if you need to sweeten the pot. Mr. Upton will make that final decision." There was no doubt in her mind on that score, she conceded silently. Mr. Yale Upton made all final decisions.

He nodded his dismissal and Hannah left, clutching the folder to her breast. It took a concentrated effort to refrain from calling Yale's office immediately for an appointment. She frowned over her yearning need to see or even to hear his voice again. The weekend had possessed some magical property, sweeping her into another orbit that she'd been helplessly unable to resist. But this was another day, and she'd always managed to separate her business and social life. Any contact she made on this case must be kept on an impersonal level.

With that firm resolve she opened the file to find his office number and placed her call. She told the secretary whom she represented and was curiously reluctant over giving her name. Would Yale think she'd asked for this assignment?

The woman knew of the search and made an appointment for the following morning. "Mr. Upton isn't in at present and his afternoon is booked solid," she explained, after asking if she had an *h* at the end of her name. "So many drop and add all sorts of letters to change the spelling," she said chattily. "I'll alert him that you'll be here at ten."

Hannah wondered achingly if she'd have to wait until then or if she'd see him that night. Nothing had been said about meeting that evening.

She went to the coffee maker and poured a cup. It was time to place a brake on her inflamed emotions. She could think this temporary infatuation into love if she weren't careful. He was everything she'd ever dreamed of in a man, and then some. But while she knew he enjoyed the lovemaking as much as she did, she was no fool. At present she was enthralled to discover she was capable of going through such a full response after the dismal attempts with her ex-fiancé. It would be wise to remember that Yale's expertise came from experience, and she'd be smart to accept right from the beginning that this affair could well be just another addition to that experience.

On that dour note she forced herself to concentrate on the letters the office boy had placed on her desk. Two held résumés from chemical engineers that she'd sent out feelers for. A large chemical company was thinking of expanding into the area and wanted to know if the talent would be available.

The other was a delayed response to a long telephone call she'd made when searching for a man to head the

Orlando operation. Her interest perked up on reading his letter. His marriage had been shaky, he admitted, and he hadn't wanted to place a strain on it at the time, but their differences had been resolved and they wanted to start in a new place.

She pulled out his folder and noted with satisfaction he could well be the man suited for Yale's expansion. Mr. Dunn, in his wisdom, had been correct again in thinking she'd be able to come up with someone suitable after her research on the other job.

The rest of the morning was spent punching the computer for other compatible candidates from their extensive morgue. In between her other work, she placed calls to the potentials to see if they were still actively interested in a change. Some had moved on already and she updated those files, but she managed to glean several hot possibilities. At least she wouldn't go empty-handed to her appointment.

By concentrating resolutely on her work, she just barely managed to remove Yale from occupying her every thought. But even when talking to others in the office, she was aware of his image sitting on the periphery ready to take over again as soon as she relaxed. The experience was totally new and even somewhat aggravating.

In spite of the rapture he'd taught her, her instincts warned her that she had to keep her private and business lives in separate compartments in order to function normally. No man had ever intruded to this devastating extent. John had noticed her vacant stare and she'd caught the quizzical look from others on the staff.

It was all too new, she admitted later when John had again embarrassingly caught her daydreaming as he'd been talking to her.

"You'd better get your act together, and either take a

cold shower or give him what he wants," he said crudely after pulling a file from her bin that he'd requested.

Hannah's face flamed in reaction as she watched him leave. He was right, of course. She had to straighten out her act, as he so succinctly put it. The question was how. Her mind warned her to place their growing affair on hold until she could cope better, but she heard her body's silent laughter. One look, one touch from him and she'd be in his arms aching to be once again consumed by his love-making.

The phone rang when she was straightening her desk for the night. Hearing the deep purr put all her vacillation to rest. Whom was she fooling? She was at Yale's beck and call for as long as he wanted her. Her destiny was in his hands.

"God, what a day," he said tiredly. "I just got out of a last conference and hoped to get you before you left. We have a dinner date in case you didn't know it."

His weariness came over the phone like a blanket, and a newfound mothering instinct took her by surprise. "You sound like you belong in bed," she protested, even as she wondered how she'd get through the night without seeing him.

"I do," he growled, "with you."

"I mean you sound terribly tired." She hoped her voice didn't give away the sensations his words shot through her.

"I guess I have cause," he admitted with a chuckle. "After all, I didn't get that much sleep this weekend, and Mondays always seem extra hectic. How did you make out?"

"More or less the same," she confessed.

A long pregnant silence hummed along the line and she found her hands becoming damp and her legs weakening under the message she was receiving.

"I'll pick you up at six," he said huskily.

"Fine," she managed. "Where will we eat?"

"I'll leave that to you. And, Hannah," his voice lowered suggestively, "it can't be soon enough for me."

"And for me," she whispered softly, reveling at the flames racing along her nerves as she slowly lowered the receiver.

Hannah stopped at the supermarket on the way home. An idea had emerged and she hurried through her shopping, intent on bringing it to blossom. Yale had sounded all too tired, and that lingering mothering instinct urged her on as she carefully selected the food. It would be much more sensible for him to relax with a home-cooked meal instead of going out, she reasoned. Her only regret was that with the limited time, she had to resort to steak again. She was a reasonably good cook and had several popular specialties that she indulged in when entertaining.

From the gourmet section, she selected two cans of gazpacho. Chilled, the Mediterranean soup would make a delightfully cool beginning on this hot summer's day. The steak would be matched with baked potatoes. She'd top them with the sour cream and crumbled bacon she already had. A spinach and tomato salad should be hearty enough, and for dessert there'd be an assortment of cheeses. Yale, she already noticed, didn't have a sweet tooth.

The buzzer rang just as she finished mixing his drink—scotch on the rocks as he liked it, with a touch of water. She gave her satin lounging pajamas a last nervous assessment. Debbie had given them to her for Christmas in her campaign to assist in rescuing her sister from the fearful prospects of spinsterhood.

The gold color was a perfect foil for her tawny hair and amber eyes. The material clung in all the right places. The neckline plunged in an alarming way, exposing the shadowed valley to inspection and giving hints of the creamy hills it separated. The back was pure seduction, with its provocative slit from neck to waist, urging masculine hands to explore the silken skin underneath. She'd never worn them before when entertaining, not wanting to have to answer to the promises it made.

But with Yale it was different, she admitted, as she flew to press the release to the entrance door. Her ears strained to the faint whirr of the elevator, when an audacious idea came to her. She ran to the bedroom and removed the shining object from the drawer. When the knock came she peered demurely past the restraining chain before releasing that last lock.

"Lost it again?" she asked pertly, dangling a key in her outstretched hand. It was an admirable repeat performance of the last devastating time he'd stormed in.

His eyes gleamed sardonically at the memory before he took the offered key and slipped it into his pants pocket. "I was wondering if you had a duplicate," he said noncommittally.

She was in his arms and his odd response was swept from her mind. "It's been at least a year," he sighed, nuzzling into the warmth of her neck. She arched to aid him in the pleasure of his exploring, but it wasn't enough. Her palms pressed against his cheeks as her hands guided his mouth to meet hers. He breathed a deep sigh before accepting her offering. It was as if he were at last home, and he drank deeply until she was an empty vessel clinging weakly to him.

He buried a hand in her hair and cushioned her head on his shoulder until the thunder of their heartbeats slowed to near normal. "Your drink," she murmured on opening her eyes and seeing the dew-covered glasses on the tray. "The ice will be all melted." Like her bones.

He released her reluctantly and handed her the weaker

one before taking an appreciative sip from his. He sat on the sofa, only then examining her with a lusting eye.

"My God, woman, where do you think I'll take you dressed like that!" he growled. "That outfit is for private consumption only!"

She pirouetted seductively before him, thrilling on seeing the lambent fires leap in his eyes. "Naturally," she admitted. "You sounded so tired, I decided we'd eat here."

She was surprised at the sound of the air being forcibly expressed from his lungs. Had he been girding for battle, thinking she intended to wear the outfit in public? The thought intrigued her, but the warning light in his eyes told her it wouldn't be wise to delve further into the matter.

Besides, on looking at him more closely over the rim of her glass she could see the lines of weariness bracketing his mouth and the telltale way he was kneading the tense muscles along his neck. She would feed him and lull him with soft music and candlelight. It must have indeed been a tough day at the office.

"The potatoes need fifteen more minutes before I put on the steak," she said. "Tell me about it. Are the problems unsolvable?"

She curled in the chair across from him. This was not the time to let the electric current that sparked between them grow too warm. Besides, she found she was enjoying playing the housewife dutifully concerned over her husband's day.

"Nothing is unsolvable," he said, finishing his drink. "Some things just take a little longer." His eyes followed her lingeringly as she rose gracefully to freshen his drink. "The day was a little hectic what with pinning down one company to accept our bid and getting their signature on the order, then telling another jobber he could you-know-what with his not so subtle inference that a little booty in his private kitty would keep the orders coming in."

He nodded his pleasure on tasting the second drink. She responded with watchful attention as he slowly unraveled under her small insertions. Only then did she go to the kitchen to put the finishing touches to the meal. She'd never known such satisfaction, she marveled. Was this what marriage was all about?

The thought stunned her, and her fingers trembled as she lit the candles before inviting him to taste the chilled soup.

It was an enchanting evening and one that ended as she never expected, she admitted ruefully when she slipped the fine English leather shoes from his feet and placed the light blanket over him.

The conversation had carried them through the meal and the clean-up that he'd insisted on helping with. He'd invited her next to him when they'd turned on the TV to listen to the President speak on the budget. They had ended stretched out on the soft cushions, Hannah lying with her back spooned against him, his hand cupped firmly over one breast, as they listened out the talk.

When the commentators rehashed what had been said, she turned her head to ask him for his evaluation. Her eyes held tender amusement upon seeing him fast asleep, the lines of weariness at last fading.

So much for a home-cooked meal and a seductive outfit! Poor Debbie would be crushed over the outcome, doubly assured her career-oriented sister was doomed.

She eased slowly away from him, pausing when his grip closed convulsively to prevent her escape. She waited until his breathing was again deep and even before slipping off the couch.

He wore a fine knit top that offered no restriction, but she bent over to open the button of his slacks. For a moment she was washed with memories of another time under very different circumstances when she'd performed the same chore.

She moved softly, putting the apartment to rights. At midnight she was torn about waking him or letting him stay the night. He'd barely moved and was still in deep sleep. Her yawn warned her she had some sleep to catch up on also, and she turned out all the lights except for the dim one in the bathroom. If he should awaken suddenly at least he could orient himself easily.

She had no idea what time it was when she roused momentarily on feeling the mattress shift. The long, strong body joined her under the sheet, drawing her close. She gave a sigh of contentment as she rubbed her cheek against his chest. The steady beat under her ear lulled her quickly back into deep sleep.

CHAPTER SEVEN

The aroma of freshly perked coffee awoke Hannah seconds before the alarm went off. Her hand went out instinctively in search of the remembered warmth that she'd been nestled against. Even in sleep, she'd been aware of him at the subconscious level. His being beside her had seemed so right.

She grabbed a robe from the closet and padded barefooted to the kitchen. He was dressed and starting the bacon, working with an economy of movements.

Her weakening knees forced her to sag against the doorway. He looked too earthshakingly gorgeous even so early in the morning.

"You'd better be careful. If you spoil me like this, I might just decide to keep you," she quipped lightly.

He turned to let his gaze smolder over her. Only then did Hannah realize that in her eager need to see him she'd selected a nylon peignoir, that, with her sheer nightgown, did nothing to hide her contours.

"And if you always look like that in the morning, I might take you up on it!" he purred. "Come here, Hannah, and properly thank me for doing maid service." He placed the spatula on the counter and stood, legs apart and hands on hips. The masculine stance matched the gleam in his eye.

The effect on her was shattering, and she flew into his arms. The kiss was long and thorough.

"Good morning, Hannah," he growled when permitting their lips to part.

The deep voice vibrated in his chest, causing her sensitized breasts to harden. She knew he felt their swelling through his thin shirt by the way his eyes darkened to almost black. His hands slid over the curve of her hips to cup her buttocks and adjust her into the cradle of his thighs. Not only her breasts had responded to that long kiss.

The bacon sputtered, causing him to mutter a soft oath. "Perhaps it's just as well," he said with reluctance. "We're both working people and I still have to get home and change."

He released his hold and turned back to his chore. "How do you like your eggs?" he asked.

Hannah had been so certain that their kiss was leading to the bed that she had to forcibly hide her disappointment. How could he dissimulate so quickly? "Once over lightly," she muttered, "and only one egg."

"I'll give you fifteen minutes," he called after her.

She shook her head in disbelief. Did he really think a woman could get ready in that short a time in the morning?

She made it in twenty minutes, just as he slid the eggs onto warmed plates and placed the crisp strips of bacon alongside them.

"You do this very well," she commented when offering him the butter for his toast.

"I worked as a short order cook one summer while in

college," he admitted. "I got so I could serve up fifty breakfasts an hour during the morning rush. One doesn't forget that lesson very quickly."

Her eyes widened. "How in the world could you do that many?"

He gave a faint shrug. "Preparation. Everything was ready and in the warmer except for the eggs. As you can imagine, it wasn't a fancy place and the menu was limited. We catered to those who were in a hurry, so we gave them what they wanted."

"Do you have a busy schedule today?" she asked, conscious of hungrily absorbing that tidbit of information he'd offered of his past before moving to another question.

"I assume so. It usually is. My secretary will tell me about it when I get in."

Hannah glanced at him with surprise. Then he didn't know about the ten o'clock appointment with her as yet! With amused perversity she decided not to tell him and topped their coffee cups, wondering what his reaction would be when he saw her name on the list.

"I apologize for fading so completely last night," he said, reaching for another slice of toast. "I guess I was more tired than I realized, but that's no excuse."

She gave a faint dismissive shrug, as if it were something she'd coped with before. "You were in a deep sleep and I didn't have the heart to awaken you."

"I went to your bedroom when I did wake up. You looked so darned comfortable and the bed looked too inviting, so I shed my clothes and crawled in." His smile was beguiling. "You're a nice quiet person to sleep with, Hannah. That is, when you're asleep."

His meaning was clear. Under his tutelage when in his arms she'd exploded in wild abandonment. His smile widened into a knowing grin. "I haven't forgotten that promised date for dinner. Tonight it will be different," he promised. "I'll expect you to be dressed to kill."

He glanced at his watch and frowned. "I'd better get moving. At least I don't have to shave. Thanks for the loan of your razor. Thank goodness it was a proper one. I hate those feminine things most women use."

Something burned around Hannah's heart. Did he make a practice of staying overnight in his current women's apartments, expecting free use of the equipment as well?

"Perhaps you should investigate the medicine cabinet before deciding about staying over," she snipped.

His eyes narrowed on seeing the withdrawn look on her face, and he gave a small sigh. "Hannah," he said gently, "I'm a man and thirty-five years old. Did you expect me to still be a virgin? I held no such illusions about you."

But she had been, practically, she wanted to shout. Instead, her lids fluttered down to hide her dismay over her senseless reaction. He was right, of course. She gave him a tremulous smile that asked for forgiveness. It had him out of the chair and pulling her to him.

She was lost immediately. The past was nothing but building blocks for the future. And the present was now, in the heaven of his arms with his lips scorching hers, giving intimate promises.

"Until tonight," he breathed against her lips. "I'll call you when I know the time I'll be finished."

He was gone and she hurriedly gave a cursory rinsing to the plates. It was late and she'd leave the washing until she returned.

At work she had barely time to return two calls that had come in early before gathering the folders of the potential candidates she'd selected and placing them in her attaché case. In a half hour she'd see Yale again, and she marveled over how that realization could send fine tremors through her.

She was barely aware of the traffic as she drove to his address, eyes bright with anticipation. Would she be pulled into his arms and rendered mindless by his kisses, or would he wait until they were through with their discussion and take her to lunch where they'd indulge in the stimulating double communication they seemed capable of, their conversation on one level while their bodies spoke in a more basic and exciting way.

The small sign on his secretary's desk said Ms. Sadie Warwick. She was a neatly dressed, middle-aged woman whose manner bespoke of quiet efficiency, which was what Hannah was certain Yale would insist upon.

"Mr. Upton is expecting you," she said in a pleasantly modulated voice. "He just called to say he's been delayed for a moment in the plant and would you mind waiting in his office."

Hannah caught her inquisitive glance and wondered if Yale had reacted in some revealing way on seeing her name on the appointment pad. More likely the woman was thinking it odd that she was admitted into the inner sanctum when he wasn't there as yet. For the first time, she wondered exactly what type electronic products he manufactured and if any of it was secret. She knew he had several government contracts.

The office was unpretentious but comfortable, and dominated by a huge ancient desk that wore its age proudly. Had he inherited it from his father? she wondered before turning her attention to the paintings on the walls.

They were Yale's additions, she was certain, and admired the seascapes, some with sailboats beating before the wind and others showing the ocean in its many moods.

She placed her case by a leather chair and brought her attention back to the desk. Her fingers trailed over the polished surface while admiring the grain of the wood. This was the nerve center of his business, and she could almost feel his presence as his alert mind wrestled with the myriad problems associated with its smooth running. The papers on the top were aligned in neat order awaiting his attention. Her gaze fastened unconsciously on the two lined sheets in the center of the blotter and a smile touched her lips. One was the list of the day's appointments and she saw her name underlined at the ten o'clock designation. He did have a full calendar, she noted, and saw with resignation that there was little likelihood they'd share a lunch together. He was already running late from whatever was holding him at the plant.

Her gaze continued over the list and a frown gathered on reading the last one. Dinner—Ms. Dorminor. But what about the dinner date he'd promised her? she protested with sudden resentment.

Her glance drifted to the other paper and recognized it as a list of telephone calls that had come in that morning. The same name leaped at her. The woman had called at eight thirty and again at nine forty-five. Who was this persistent Ms. Dorminor who felt free to call Yale at his office?

She moved away from the desk to stare bleakly out of the window. Her arms crossed over her chest to ease the pain building within. What did she know about Yale's personal life? she wondered dully. She had been swamped by his masculine charisma. *I am a man,* he had said when he thought she'd questioned his past. She pressed her forehead against the cool glass as if the pressure could stop her whirling thoughts. There was Theda and now this Dorminor woman. How many more names would come up to haunt her, and, dear Lord, how was she going to cope?

The confused resentment that had been hers when she

had found out about her fiancé's amorous activities returned. She had vowed that she'd never be placed in that humiliating and confidence-destroying position again. But what she was feeling now hit with a deeper intensity and she knew why.

Jealousy was a new emotion to her, and she admitted she didn't like what it was doing to her. She wanted to run and hide until she could find the weapons to combat its corroding action. One thing she knew, she had no desire to see Yale at present until she could pull herself together.

"Sorry to keep you waiting, Hannah," he said from the door. "A problem in control came up and I had to see to it immediately."

He stood tall and vital as his eyes smoked messages of past and future pleasures. Why did he have to look so magnificent? she agonized. It wasn't fair that one man could have such control over her senses that just seeing him had her trembling. She admitted to a sympathy for all the women he'd held in his power. How could she be jealous of them, knowing they must have felt as helpless as she did when subjected to his magnetism.

"That's understandable," she managed to say in a cool, dismissive voice. *Tell me who she is!* she wanted to scream. *Why is she so important that she's usurping our dinner date?*

Somehow she managed to keep her expression under careful control as she went swiftly to pick up her case by the chair and sat down. "I can understand your tight schedule, so I won't waste your time." She withdrew the file from the case and became the efficient businesswoman, ignoring the sick feeling gnawing in her middle.

Yale's gaze was quizzical before he took his place behind the desk. Hannah kept her head bent as she sorted through the papers. From his stance, she knew he had expected her to fly into his arms and be greeted with a kiss, and all of her ached over her refusal to do so.

She started immediately on the reason for the appointment, stating she needed more in-depth information on just what he expected in the way of a background for the supervisor and what he had to offer.

He gave her a probing look, as if to see the reason behind her behavior before deciding to go along with her act.

Previously they'd discussed his problem in generalities, but now she was exposed to the keenly honed businessman who had built his company to its present prestigious level and intended to carry it to its upper limits. The controlled power she had only suspected was now exposed to her full viewing, and she felt a surge of longing to be the one privileged to be by his side as he made his advance up the ladder.

"I do have three men who might fill your requirements," she said, handing him their files. "I can set up appointments with you at your convenience. Meanwhile we'll continue to put out feelers for other likely candidates."

His inspection was quick but thorough. One he rejected immediately and the other two he agreed to see.

The amber light on the intercom blinked and he pressed the release. "Ms. Dorminor is on the phone," his secretary announced. "She's called twice this morning."

Hannah stiffened on hearing the name. She'd managed to bury her feelings while concentrating on her presentation, but now they returned unabated in their sharpness.

She watched for a change of expression with hawklike intensity, but the controlled mask he'd assumed after her cool greeting remained unchanged.

"Excuse me," he said politely before depressing the button to accept the call. He lifted the receiver and turned his swivel chair until he was looking out of the expanse of window behind him.

Hannah bit her lip as she stared at the back of his head. Had he deliberately done that so she wouldn't see any slip in his expression as they talked? The pain was almost intolerable in her chest, and she carefully took a deep breath to lessen it.

It was apparent that Yale knew the woman, and well. His voice was the low purring rumble that wreaked such havoc to her senses. The opening conversation was about mutual friends before she evidently told of the reason for her call. He turned back to the desk and frowned slightly when picking up the sheet listing his appointments. "Of course I haven't forgotten, Lois," he said. "I'll see you at seven."

Hannah flinched on hearing the words. Until then she'd been certain he'd cancel the appointment when seeing the conflict, but she was the one being canceled out.

She snapped the case shut and stood up when he was through. "I believe that covers everything so far," she said. "I'll get back to you about when to set up the appointments, so you can meet the men."

Yale rose, and she hurried to the door before he could make any contact. If he touched her, she was afraid she'd burst into tears and the thought horrified her. She paused at the door, a tight distant smile on her lips. "By the way, when I got to the office I saw in my appointment book that I have a previous engagement for tonight. Perhaps we can make it sometime in the future when we both have some free time . . ."

She fled, the surge of anger on his face causing a sudden apprehension to hit her. She was safe in his office with all his personnel around, for heaven's sake, she reasoned. But on second thought a doubt rose. When angry, he was all too likely to take matters in his own hands.

She hurried to her car and sped out of the parking lot. Not until she put distance between them did the fear of being pursued ease. She had to stop acting so irrational, she scolded herself, then admitted grimly that ever since meeting Yale, her every action had been just that, from falling so abandoningly into his arms to giving him the key to her apartment. A frown lined a crease between the delicately curved eyebrows on remembering his cool acceptance of the key and the fleeting but odd expression. He'd have no way of knowing he was the first to own one, and she wished she'd told him so. Had he thought she did that often?

Not like he did, she glowered, envisioning a line of sophisticated beauties, each with his key in her possession. The ache returned to her chest over the thought that Theda had been one of the privileged and no doubt the just as stunningly attractive Lois Dorminor. After all, she'd just found out a dinner date with the woman held preference over one with her.

By the time she made her report to Mr. Dunn it was time for lunch but she had no desire to eat. Instead, she spent the rest of the afternoon making long distance calls, following up leads on possibilities that might meet Yale's requirements. She wished she had the courage to ask Mr. Dunn to take her off the case, but she quailed on being subjected to his piercing inspection. Those all-seeing eyes would see too much, and her emotions where Yale was concerned were still too raw for any exposure. She left the office early, unable to concentrate on working further.

When she reached her apartment, she was too restless to sit down. The blanket at the end of the sofa brought back in vivid detail how she'd nestled against Yale and later covered him so tenderly with it. There'd been no time to make the bed and the pillow still held the imprint of his head that had rested so close to hers. By the time she reached the kitchen and saw the stacked dishes, reminding her of the intimate breakfast they'd shared, she was a basket case. Every room was haunted by his presence, and it was more than she could take.

In desperation, she pulled on jeans and a faded T-shirt and grabbed an old Windbreaker and escaped to the beach. On reaching the sand, she rolled up the pant legs and placed her sneakers in the pockets of her jacket. These solitary runs had always soothed her and, if she expected to sleep that night, she was in desperate need of that tranquilizing effect. The sun set in orange splendor and she huddled in the jacket when the breeze cooled. She felt better, she admitted, when reaching her car, but it was still too early and she didn't want to face the haunted emptiness of her apartment.

She drove to the movie theater in the mall, deciding to lose herself in the highly acclaimed science fiction movie being featured. Surely by that time she'd be tired enough to creep home and fall into bed.

The movie had received excellent reviews, but it was wasted on her. Her mind was too full of the evening with Yale that hadn't materialized. He'd told her to dress to kill and she had felt an excitement as if he intended it to be something special. Was it being special with his Lois Dorminor? she wondered bitterly.

She forced herself to remain until the end and straggled out with the crowd. When she reached the door she was greeted by several old school friends and was invited to join them for a pizza and beer. Why not? she thought. Maybe they'd be able to jolt her out of her depressing mood.

It wasn't successful, and she left before ten, pleading a busy schedule at work the next day. Their chatter had seemed flighty and meaningless when held in comparison to the stimulating range of subjects she'd enjoyed with

Yale. She gave a dejected sigh after she had pulled into her apartment parking lot and locked her car. She'd made him unnecessarily angry with her parting words and she doubted his male ego would permit him to consider contacting her again. Why should he when he had his Thedas and Loises eager to fawn over him? Besides, her action had left him in little doubt that she didn't want to see him again.

She double-locked her door before moving despondently into the living room, there to freeze.

"Where the devil have you been!" Yale grated from the sofa.

Hannah's first reaction of joy on his being there was immediately replaced by one of fear on seeing the anger on his face. She backed prudently against the wall while eyeing a possible escape route to the bedroom. She gave up that idea at once. He might look deceptively sprawled in relaxation on the couch, but she sensed the coiled muscles ready to spring.

Her tongue went nervously over dry lips as she tried to convince herself the best offence was a defense. "Out, where else would I be?" she said smartly. "I told you I had an appointment."

His eyes started at her sneakers and moved with narrowed evaluation over her faded jeans and shirt and to the wind-tousled hair. Only now did she recall she hadn't stopped at the rest room in the theater as planned to repair the damage done by her walk on the beach.

In contrast, he looked elegantly debonair. His white formal jacket was tossed on the sofa beside him and his tie had been removed, but the thin linen shirt with finely tucked pleats, the black trousers, and patent leather shoes were devastatingly attractive on him.

For the first time, she noticed the bottle of scotch on the coffee table. It had been reduced by several inches, and she looked at him with mounting apprehension. She had no idea what he'd be like when inebriated. When cold sober his anger was formidable enough.

"It looks like he gave you a thorough going-over," he snarled, watching her attempt to comb her fingers through her tangled hair.

Her chin went up. "I was walking on the beach," she said tightly. If he assumed someone had been with her, it was his own fault for prejudging her.

He leaned forward to place his glass on the table with careful precision. "Did seeing my car warn you not to invite him here?"

"If I'd seen your car, *I* wouldn't be here!" she shot back. He looked poised to strike and she looked around in desperation for something to protect herself with.

He stared at her for a long moment, sending her agitation into a new high. "I'd like the true story now on why you canceled our date."

It wasn't the question she expected and she blinked in surprise. "I told you . . ."

"I don't like liars," he cut in sharply. "When I finally got my schedule under control this afternoon, I went to your office to see what in the world was bugging you this morning. You were so uptight, I thought you'd split. The receptionist wasn't at her desk, and when I saw the door with your name on it, I went to see if you were there. You weren't, but your appointment book was. There was no engagement listed for the evening."

Hannah felt the heat rise to her cheeks. In her angry embarrassment, she made a last attempt to take the offensive position again. "You had no right to invade my privacy! And, besides, what are you so upset about? It eliminated your need to break our date so you could go out with your Miss Dorminor!"

A black brow arched for a second before a faint smile

appeared. She blinked over the sudden cessation of the tension filling the room. "Do I detect a little green in those remarkable eyes again?"

She was thrown off center by the abrupt absence of antagonism. He was actually purring. "I see no reason why you should assume that unless your ego demands it," she spat out. She couldn't believe that he was actually enjoying her discomfort.

He stood up and she retreated back to the wall. "Come here, you foolish woman," he ordered, his eyes sending the smoky signals she could never resist. "We're wasting time when we have more important things to do."

She watched him warily as he took two strides toward her. The anger was definitely gone and she barely hesitated before going eagerly into his arms. She was beyond fooling herself that she should resist him when that was where she wanted to be.

"What am I going to do about you?" he said musingly, his mouth making small forays over her face and throat. "I have to do something about what you do to my blood pressure when trying to decipher what that fertile imagination of yours is conjuring up next."

She only half-heard his words as she longed with increased hunger for his mouth to find the path to her waiting lips. She had thought she'd never be in his arms again, pressed against his warm firm body and her happiness became a delirium of delight when he at last claimed possession.

"Mmm, pizza," he murmured after his first brush of her lips.

"And scotch," she returned. "I see you like the house label."

"I'll take any label you're using," he said suggestively, recapturing her mouth and letting his tongue communicate how much he was enjoying it.

Each kiss had seemed the ultimate in rapture, but this one shook her to her core. There was a fierce possession and remnants of his anger, but under it lay a bottomless hunger that compelled her to pour her soul into her response.

A moan rose in her throat when his hand closed over her breast. Reacting unconsciously, her hips rotated against his, activating a groan that rumbled in his chest.

"Vixen!" he growled before taking her lips in renewed passion. His free hand cupped her bottom, alerting her to the reason for his anchoring her to his thighs. They strained to each other until kisses weren't enough.

They tore at each other's clothes with frantic urgency and sank to the plush carpet wrapped in each other's arms.

It was a quick mating, explosive and necessary to drain the last of the residual anger and frustration. "You're something else again," he said with a disbelieving glance over the thick carpet. "I thought I was too old for this type of lovemaking, but you keep managing to drive me crazy."

Their damp bodies parted reluctantly and, taking her hand, he drew her up with him. "Next time we do it properly and in bed," he said with a faint leer. "Meanwhile, feed me something, woman."

"You mean your advanced age forces you to take time out to restoke the furnace?" she asked saucily.

The roar came up from his chest. "You're asking for it!" he warned, coming after her, but Hannah escaped, giggling, to the bathroom to take a quick shower and return shortly wrapped modestly in a bathrobe.

"I thought you had been out to dinner," she said when they sat down to a hurriedly made omelet and thick slices of Italian bread.

He gave her a lowering glare. "I was, but I wasn't hungry at the time."

She lowered her lashes demurely. Was she the cause for

the lost appetite? She'd barely nibbled at the pizza herself when with her friends.

If she thought his probing was over, she underrated the determined man. His questioning resumed later when she was tucked next to him in the bed. "How did you spend the evening?" he asked softly, his attention focused on the reaction of her nipple as he traced lazy circles around the aureole and smiled with male satisfaction at the instant erection to the blatant tease. She barely suppressed the responsive wriggle as she attempted to prove she could maintain an immunity to his seduction.

"The ocean was calm and it was ideal for a run on the beach." She wasn't about to let him know she was by herself.

But he wasn't letting her get away with that vague statement. "Who was with you?"

"Did there have to be someone?" she asked provocatively.

"Who?" he persisted.

"There was the movies later and then we tried a new pizza parlor," she said, careful to stay within the framework of the truth.

"Hannah!" He gave a warning tug on the hardened tip.

"What difference does it make whom I might have been with!" she cried in rising irritation.

He rose swiftly above her to rest his elbows on either side of her shoulders. "I'll tell you what difference it makes," he said harshly.

His hands cupped her face, forcing her to meet the stormy swirling in his eyes. She lay still, her heart pounding heavily under the unexpected menace he projected.

"I thought you understood the rules," he grated, grim lines pulling at the corners of his mouth. "As long as this affair lasts, there's to be no other man in your life."

Anger rescued her. "How dare you give me ultimatums!" she stormed. "You know what you can do with any affair if you think you can take control over me. You can go now and leave the key on your way out. I realize now I was a fool to give it to you. You seem to assume it gives you the right to lead my life. Well, I'm telling you, you're way off. Take your clothes and get out of here, damn you! Go back to your Lois Dorminor. Maybe she'll take your ordering! If you can go out with whom you please, how dare you question whom I go with?"

She was incensed and shouting when finished, and writhing against him, trying to break out of his grip.

As before, when mentioning the woman's name, his body lost its tautness and he let its weight halt her struggling. "You're a fiery little witch when angry, aren't you?" he purred, and the accompanying chuckle put an effective halt to her attempt to break free.

She looked at him in bewilderment, unable to grasp the reason for the sudden change in his temper. She was breathing heavily from her struggling and he glanced down in fascination at the action of her breasts against the hair covering his chest.

The chuckle became a groan. "Witch, vixen, they all fit you. Do you know what that does to me?"

His body slid down over hers until his face was buried in the bewitching valley before tasting one, then the other of the hardening peaks, nipping, licking, suckling them into tingling response.

He slid lower, drawing his slightly bristly jaw along the smoothness of her abdomen, roughing the tender skin before soothing it with hot, moist kisses until her nerve endings quivered to the heady stimuli. Her hands kneaded restlessly over the muscles banding his shoulders, urging him on in his quest. By the time he repeated the process on the sensitive area of her inner thighs, her body convoluted in exquisite spasms that had her calling his name in supplication. "Yale . . . please . . . I can't take any more."

Slowly he retraced his path until he again found the rich territory in her mouth. She arched her hips to meet his full possession, matching eagerly the rhythm he started, aching for the release only he could give before she went up in fire.

They spiraled up until there was no thought except the beauty of the rapture their bodies were giving them. When they reached the pinnacle, there was only the outer darkness, the ultimate fulfillment to fly into, then the slow spiral down again until Hannah realized she had been anchored safely through it all in the protection of his arms.

"Yale," she murmured drowsily minutes later. She was drawn with her back to him, her contours melded to his, and his arms holding her firmly in place. "I have a confession to make. I had no date tonight. There was no man."

"Hush, sweet heart," he replied, placing a last kiss behind her ear. "I know."

It wasn't until almost asleep that the vagrant thought reached her. Yale had never confessed who Lois Dorminor was, or why a date with her had held priority. She'd have to ask him about her at breakfast. There must be a sensible answer. He'd demanded trust, and in the aftermath of what they'd just shared, it was easy to give.

CHAPTER EIGHT

There was no time the next morning to question Yale as planned. They had forgotten to set the alarm and in the rush to get off, they had time for only a quick cup of coffee and toast as they took turns using the shower.

"I'll see you tonight," he promised when kissing her after seeing her to her car before taking off in his, and she promised herself she'd have an answer to the nagging question that night.

Her workload kept her busy through the morning and she welcomed the lunch date she'd made with a client. She'd found that men, when reaching the executive level, invariably were ill at ease when placed in the position of being interviewed. They were used to sitting on the other side of the desk. Eating in an elegant restaurant was much more relaxing for them and Hannah had found the atmosphere also gave her the opportunity to evaluate the subtle nuances of their personalities which frequently made for a more satisfactory placement.

Mr. Baker proved to be the kind of man she loved to interview. He was approaching his sixties, with graying temples and a polished surface. He carried himself with the distinction that came from being well versed in leadership. He was a vice-president of a large corporation and realized he had little chance of going any higher and felt stagnant. As a result, he was toying with the idea that being the big chief in a smaller company might offer more of a challenge at this time of life.

She took him to Bentley's, a restaurant in West Palm Beach that featured unobtrusive service along with a select menu. The interior was divided into smaller rooms with a limited number of tables which gave the customers an aura of privacy.

Mr. Baker proved to be a connoisseur of wines, and she was happy to leave the selection to him. It was a pleasant change from the usual double martini gambit.

Hannah was pleased with the result of the interview, confident they'd be able to match him with the type position he'd like. "You might have to take a cut in salary," she warned him. Small companies were hard pressed to meet wages offered by huge conglomerates.

He nodded his acceptance. "I've accrued enough stock over the years in bonuses so that won't bother me. Of course, I have my limits to what I'll take, but if the challenge is there, I admit I'll be tempted."

The rooms had partial window-size openings between them to give a feeling of open space. The apertures held interesting pieces of sculpture and they were discussing the merits of the one opposite them while waiting for the check when Hannah gave a faint gasp and fought the fleeting blackness that swirled before her eyes.

The couple who had just entered the adjacent room were Yale and a striking brunette. She was almost as tall as he and, from the way their heads were bent to each other, they were old acquaintances. His arm went around her shoulders when the woman gazed up at him and Hannah watched with an agonizing bitterness when his mouth brushed hers. She accepted the chair the waiter was holding for her and they sat down and disappeared from view behind the shoulder-high wall that separated the rooms.

Hannah felt violently sick and gulped desperately to fight the weakness swamping her. The palms of her hands were damp and she knew there was a pearling on her upper lip also. She reached for her wineglass with both hands so the trembling wouldn't be apparent, and drained the contents in thirsty gulps.

She was thankful Mr. Baker's interest was still on the decorations. By the time the check arrived, she had a modicum of control over herself and managed to function with surface normalcy until she was back in the office.

Once safe behind her closed door, she couldn't still the trembling that she'd been holding at bay. She fought the aftermath of shock by trying to put what she saw into proper focus. She'd been out with a personable man, hadn't she? Why couldn't Yale's have been a business appointment also?

But it wasn't, she knew. They had projected a sense of intimacy that only a close association could give. She had wondered if she'd be exposed to more of his past affairs besides Theda and that Lois Dorminor. It was apparent the brunette was another, and the jealousy that had simmered over the unknown woman flared into a new violence.

Dear God, she wailed, if it hurt this much after knowing him only a short time, how bad would the pain be when he finally became tired of her?

A surging anger came to her rescue. So he was working on the old double standard, was he! she stormed. As with her former fiancé, she evidently was supposed to acquiesce to his demand to remain true to him while he continued with his little affairs on the side. Like a fool, she had thought he was giving the same commitment to her. She never played the field, in fact she'd abdicated playing in that fast lane after her disastrous engagement.

A new pain shot through her on recalling how easily he'd battered down her defenses and, having taught the ultimate rapture of mutual fulfillment, she'd been putty in his hands.

She gave a groan as she buried her head in her arms, fighting the tears, knowing how they reddened her eyes. She still had to pass under the scrutiny of the personnel in the outer office. And she cringed on thinking what their comments would be after she left.

She jerked her head up when John, with only a cursory knock, came into the office. His lips pursed on seeing her pale, strained expression.

"You look lousy," he said bluntly. "What gives? Having a migraine or something?"

Her head was pounding unmercifully and she nodded weakly. "It must be a reaction to the wine I had at lunch." She gave the excuse, having read recently that it had that effect on some people.

"I came in to see if you'd typed the rundown on Baker as yet," he said, accepting her excuse without further comment. "I think I have a position opening up that might be right for him. But it can wait until tomorrow. Why don't you go home and take some aspirin and crawl into bed. It looks like that's where you belong."

It was where she longed to be and she apologized after giving him the highlights of her interview. "I'll have the full report on your desk tomorrow," she promised.

She stopped briefly to tell Helen, who monitored the switchboard and front desk, to hold all her calls. "Tell them I'll get back to them in the morning," she said, and left, feeling a fraud over the girl's sympathetic offerings of remedies to try.

But her head was killing her and she gave a grateful sigh on reaching her apartment, anxious for the oblivion of sleep. Tomorrow would be soon enough to figure out what to do next. Her fingers gripped in spasm on the door frame as she stared at the bed. They had awakened late that morning and there'd been no time to make it up. She'd folded the sheets back to air the bed, but her gaze was fixed hypnotically on the two pillows, each still holding an indentation from their heads. She screwed her lids shut against the visions of the heady passion that had been shared less than twenty-four hours before. There'd be no rest, tortured by the memories and enveloped by the lingering musky smell that was part of his lovemaking. Even if she changed the sheets, she knew she was in no condition to find sleep there.

She went to the closet to pull out her overnight bag. Letta always kept her room ready at home and she longed to escape there. Perhaps in the room that had cradled her through a happy childhood she might be able to again recapture some of its innocent tranquility.

The throbbing in her head warned her she needed some aspirin if she intended to do any driving. She pressed her hands against her pounding temples on returning from the bathroom and knew until the pills took effect, she had to lie down. She shed her clothes in a pained daze and slipped into bed, instinctively curling into a ball where Yale's long body had lain, and buried her face into the pillow that had cushioned his head. Tears trickled silently from the corners of her eyes, and dried as she sank into a deep exhausted sleep.

A gentle hand brushed strands of hair from her cheek, and she turned her face to place a kiss in his palm. Only one hand had that special touch and she smiled in drowsy contentment, her body stretching and arching in feline grace as it waited for further caresses.

"What's the matter, sweet heart?" The deep voice questioned softly. "They said at the office that you left early and weren't feeling well."

Her eyes flew open and her body stiffened as memory flooded back. "How did you get in here?" she demanded. He had no right to be sitting on her bed, her body all too ready to absorb the heat emanating from his.

"You gave me a key, remember?" he asked, a smile softening the firm set to his mouth. "What happened, honey? Has last night's activities taken their toll? If it would make you feel any better, I admit to dragging a little today also." The smile broadened into a sensuous outline.

His hand had moved slowly in caressing strokes over her shoulder and was cupping the curve of her breasts. Smoke swirled in his eyes in awareness that she had no clothes on under the sheet. She slithered across the bed to the far side and stared at him in rising anger. How dare he try the seduction scene on her after wining and dining one of his mistresses!

"Since you're here, I can't throw you out, but will you please leave the room so I can get dressed?" she said coldly.

His surprise was quickly masked as he examined her stony face for a long moment before he rose and stared down at her. "I don't know what's biting your tail now, but I guess we'll have to thrash it out," he said with a sigh of resignation.

Watching his broad back leave the room, she felt a perverse resentment that he'd offered no further argument, especially since she was keyed up to have one. Hurriedly pulling on jeans and a loose-fitting shirt, she refused to acknowledge that part of the resentment was because he'd left without the struggle she'd anticipated after seeing the smoky fire ignited in his eyes. Was he already tired of her and admitting to a lack of interest to pursue her further? Last night he'd swept her into his arms, giving her no opportunity to object.

Skittering from the irritating thought, she brushed her hair with harsh strokes. She decided against lipstick and refused to check her appearance in the mirror. She had no intention of looking like a sex object while ripping off a few home truths at him.

She paused at the door in spite of the irrational anger. Her quick temper was known to melt away as rapidly as it flared and she needed its protection to carry her through what she knew had to be done. She was aware that one touch and she'd be in his arms and hating herself afterward for not having the strength to resist him. What did he have to do—actually bed one of his women before her very eyes before she could break this hold he had on her, she grumbled in fleeting disgust. She held as a shield the picture of him hugging the brunette close before kissing her, uncaring if the whole world saw how much she meant to him. Then Hannah opened the door, her chin set at a belligerent angle.

He was outlined by the window, staring at the skyline, but turned on hearing her enter. He had discarded the jacket to his business suit and loosened his tie and she had to tear her gaze from the broad shoulders as memories of how perfectly her head had nestled there crowded in on her. He stepped toward her, an anticipatory smile on his lips, and she hurriedly moved to place a chair between them, afraid to allow him to come nearer. Just to breathe his heady scent would make it impossible to concentrate on what had to be said.

He stopped, his stance aggressively wide-legged. His thumbs hooked over his belt as he studied her with silvered eyes. "All right, what is it this time?" he asked with patient indulgence.

There was no way she could tell him about having seen the amorous scene in the restaurant. He'd accused her too often of being prey to the green-eyed monster and she wasn't about to feed his ego again.

"I've been thinking about us," she started hurriedly. "About our . . . our . . ."

"Affair," he supplied bluntly.

She nodded, submerging the pain at his admission that that was all their sharing was to him. Why it should hurt, she didn't know. He'd been explicit enough about that being all he wanted.

"I've been having second thoughts," she continued doggedly, "and I feel that we're moving too fast. After all, we've known each other for only two weeks, and I don't feel ready to make the commitment you're asking of me. I did have a satisfactory life-style before, and I see no reason why I have to cancel other friends simply because your ego demands it." She glared at him in defiance and almost gasped in shock at the naked anger expressed on his face. She should have remembered how threatening it could be. Her fingers gripped the back of the chair as if needing its protection as his fury seemed to expand until the room vibrated with it.

"What are you looking for, a session of juvenile handholding and sweet talk while you overcome your girlish vacillating?" His silky voice was more forbidding because of the tight control it exhibited.

"Yes . . . no . . ." What did she want? she wondered in sudden confusion, and realized she should have thought out her rebellion more clearly before leaving herself open to his demolition.

"I don't know what merry chase you like to lead your so-called friends on, but you'd better think twice before you assume I'm willing to dangle while you blow hot and cold. We've traveled long past that stage. I'm a man and I won't tolerate anything less than a woman in every sense of the word. If you find that's too much of a commitment to make, then it's time we said good-bye."

He glared at her, demanding her obedience to his will. Afterward she knew that if he hadn't appeared so domineeringly assured of her compliance or had made even one conciliatory gesture, she'd have capitulated and flown into his arms. She had expected him to play along with her whim, knowing full well it couldn't have lasted after knowing the wonder of his lovemaking. All she had wanted was the breathing space until she had the opportunity to impress on him that she was willing to stay true to him as long as he did the same. Instead, he was issuing his ultimatum and her pride made her retaliate with one of her own.

"Then I think you'd better leave," she said with a cool dismissal that surprised her. "We evidently have nothing further to say."

She was frozen under his icy stare. His thumbs unhooked from his belt and with studied deliberation his hand slid into his pocket to withdraw a leather case. He selected a shiny metal key and unsnapped it before placing it on the end table next to him.

"I assume you know what you're doing," he said in a hard, flat voice. "When you grow up and change your mind, you know where to contact me." He reached for his jacket and moved past her. The door closed behind him with the finality of a death knell.

Hannah began to shiver uncontrollably, her fingers pressed in spasms on the back of the chair. Dear God in heaven, what had she done! She stood there, unable to move for what seemed like an eon in time, her ears straining for the intercom to buzz, alerting her that he had returned as he'd done that first time.

When there was no more hope that he was repeating that action, she unfastened her fingers, aching from the strain placed on them. With an unsteady gait she went to the kitchen and started the water for coffee. Her insides felt frozen and she craved its heat. Fool, fool, fool! she berated herself, but felt too confused to do any coherent thinking.

She carried the mug clutched in both hands for its warmth and went into the living room to sink into a chair. She sipped the steaming liquid mindlessly until she realized she was staring at the rug where they'd exploded in that first exchange of passion before repeating it in bed in a slower and more explicit sharing.

The mug clattered to the table and she dashed to the bedroom as if hoping to outpace the pain that was finally breaking through. But his ghost was there also, standing in gloriously unashamed nakedness for her inspection as they undressed each other, and lying entwined in each other's arms as they whispered enticing words of endearment that had added to their spiraling rapture. Realizing there was no place in her apartment that she could get away from his haunting presence, she collapsed helplessly on the bed, unable to hide any longer from the horror of what she had precipitated.

Sleep came late but fitfully. She woke up the next morning clutching the pillow Yale had slept on. She stared unbelievingly at the haggard face reflected in the mirror. This had to stop, she scolded herself. If, no, *when* Yale called in the afternoon, she quickly amended, she'd have to look her best. It wouldn't do to let him see the effect he could have over her.

It was a new day and under the brilliance of the sunshine she was seeing her actions in a new light. Yale had asked for trust and she'd given him a childish ultimatum. What, after all, had she to base her case on? A seductive Theda whom Yale had indicated was in the past, whatever their relationship might have been at one time. An unknown Lois Dorminor, who could have been a business acquaintance. He'd told her enough about his intricate dealings for contracts that it could well be possible. As for the stunning brunette, she forcibly reviewed what she'd seen. True he'd hugged her to him, but the kiss had been placed on her cheek, she saw with new clarity, not on her lips! Had she made some dreadful mistake, abetted by the new emotion called jealousy?

She felt almost human after a stinging shower and carefully applied makeup. On the way to work she vowed she'd act properly subdued when he read his spiel over her, and her imagination played with a sensuous relish over how she'd make it up to him afterward.

When she finished the result of her interview with Mr. Baker, she had it duplicated for insertion into the computer and carried a copy to John. He took it from her with a grunt of thanks while eyeing her appreciatively.

"The rest seems to have done its job," he commented before checking the report to see if he needed anything clarified. "I'll include him in my file of probables," he said with satisfaction. "By the way, I might have one that will fill the bill for that Upton job." He rummaged through the pile on his desk and extracted a folder. "I interviewed him a few days ago and haven't had time as yet to punch him into the morgue, so I know you don't have him."

Hannah nodded her thanks. She ran a practiced eye over the man's résumé and knew instinctively that he fitted Yale's exacting requirements. Her first impulse was to set up an immediate appointment and carry it triumphantly to him. It would be a perfect way to smooth the waters for their meeting. She didn't know what stayed her hand, perhaps some perverse need for him to make the first move.

A strained look appeared around her eyes as the afternoon drew to a close. There'd been no purring voice on the phone asking when she would be through. Perhaps he'd had an exceptionally busy day, she rationalized. If she hit the speed limit, she should be home in plenty of time to get his call there. Should she prepare another dinner for him like the night he'd come so exhausted? They could talk then over coffee in the circle of his arms.

The long summer's day turned into velvet darkness. Hannah stared unseeingly out the window, her hands gripping the frame. If she counted to one hundred slowly, surely by then . . .

A low whimper lay in her throat. Whom was she fooling? All day she had played this game, pretending that he would call. She'd done it up brown this time, vacillating like the child he accused her of being. He didn't reach thirty-five and the place he'd carved for himself in the business world by tolerating fools. There were too many women in the world willing to give what he wanted and too wise to duplicate her stupidity once they'd tasted the bliss offered in his arms. Why should he be bothered with her moods?

When she wearily snapped out the lights she flinched on seeing the key still lying on the table where he'd placed it. It glinted, a malevolent eye staring condemningly at her, to haunt her in repeated nightmares throughout the night.

CHAPTER NINE

The week drew to a dreary close and Hannah found herself standing before Mr. Dunn's office door, drawing in a deep breath before raising her hand to knock.

There'd been no contact from Yale. As far as she knew, he could have disappeared from the face of the earth. It had been a miserable week with her vacillating between anger at him for his neglect and a desperation over what the empty nights were doing to her.

Surely a simple request to cool their ardor until they knew each other better shouldn't have caused him to withdraw like this. Before, he had stormed her portals, showing how pitifully inadequate was her resistance to him. Why this about-face? Even confronting his anger was better than this void created by his retreat.

The increasing loose fit of her clothes warned she had to do something about her lack of appetite, and it was reaching a point where her carefully applied makeup barely hid the shadows caused by dream-tossed nights that gave her little rest. And the increasing guarded looks from the office personnel told of a temper attached to a short fuse.

She grasped the folder in her hand more tightly and gave a short rap on the door. She wasn't looking forward to the next few minutes, but it had to be done. Yale's file had lain like a time bomb on her desk and she finally accepted that the only way to successfully banish him from her mind and get on with the routine of living was to remove all trace of him from her life.

The deep bass voice called her in and she straightened her shoulders before entering Mr. Dunn's inner sanctum.

"I have a request to make, Mr. Dunn," she started, placing the folder on his desk. "I find it necessary to withdraw from handling this case and would like to suggest it be transferred to John."

His massive form shifted as he leaned back in the swivel chair, his heavy brows lowering as he impaled her with his piercing blue eyes. "Sit down and tell me the problem," he said without a trace of the expected surprise.

She sank gratefully into the chair and forced herself to meet his inspection. "Actually there's no problem. I just think Mr. Upton will relate better to John." If he'd interpret her words that he was one of those chauvinists who disliked dealing with women in business, so much the better.

She sat unmoving under his evaluation as his gaze observed the hollow cheeks and shadowed eyes and no doubt guessed at the weight loss from the loose hang of the suit she wore. It was well known that those all-seeing eyes never missed anything.

"As you know, there are times when two people don't quite mesh and I thought it best for the company if I withdrew now at the outset so John can carry on. I can fill him in on what I've done to date." She was proud that her voice showed none of her nervousness over her twisting of the facts.

"Did he make a pass at you?" he asked bluntly.

She almost laughed hysterically at the unexpected question. Pass? He'd walked in and had taken full possession of her. She had no idea of the pain and vulnerability betrayed by her expressive eyes.

He leaned forward to pick up the folder. "All right, if that's what you want," he said gruffly as he handed it back to her. "You'd better give this to John and fill him in, then tell him to report back to me."

She was too relieved to do more than nod gratefully. She'd been keyed up for more searching questions and had been marshalling her defenses all day for this confrontation. Mr. Dunn didn't tolerate fools, and she was acting foolish in permitting her personal life to interfere with her business commitments. But there was no way she could sit calmly in the office with Yale when going over the reports and act as if there'd been nothing between them. She buried herself in her work the following week, seeking the exhaustion it gave her.

"Do you mind telling me what's bugging you?" John demanded after overhearing her lace into a typist for bringing her a report that proved incomplete. "You're working hard for the title of Miss Ugly. The poor girl can only fill in the information that's given to her. I've been hearing grumbles, and if you don't let up on them, we'll have no one willing to work for us."

A flush stained her cheeks as she stared down at the pen grasped tightly in her hand. She forced herself to relax the stranglehold and only then realized how that same tension had possession of her whole body. What was happening to her? she wondered in confusion. She'd always had a good rapport with her coworkers. Why was she lashing out at everyone?

She raised tear-sheened eyes that had John patting her shoulder awkwardly in sudden concern. "It's okay, Hannah," he said gruffly. "We all have lows we have to climb out of. Perhaps you should take a short vacation. I don't think you've been really up to par since you had the flu."

His solicitous attitude had her swallowing around the lump in her throat. "I'll be all right," she managed.

"You've been tied to the desk too long. What you need is a change of pace," he continued with brotherly concern. "You've been putting the rest of us to shame with the work you've been turning out. With the weekend coming up, why don't you proclaim a holiday and laze on the beach or talk your boyfriend into taking you water skiing or something."

She gave him a forced smile. "A good idea. I'll see if I can scare up a game of tennis." He could be right, she conceded. The physical activity might be the change she needed to help pull herself together.

She called her father after John left and he happily agreed to tennis and lunch afterward at the club. "I was going to get in touch with you," he said. "I haven't seen you on the courts for a good two months. Can't have you going soft on me!"

He quickly hid his concern when meeting her outside the locker rooms the next morning. The pert white tennis dress with its edging of narrow scarlet braid couldn't hide the new slenderness, and the bright sunlight gave extra shadows to the hollows in the curves of her cheeks.

His anxiety increased when he sensed her tiring before the set was through. Hannah had always been a challenging tennis player, able to keep up with most of the men, so when her returns started falling short, he wondered over the cause of the weight loss.

"I certainly was a disaster," she apologized with a forced laugh while wiping her face with the towel he handed her. "I didn't know I could deteriorate to such an extent in such a short time."

He signaled to the waiter as he led her across the patio to a shaded table. "Mind telling me what's happened to you?" he asked gently after ordering their usual tonic.

"Whatever do you mean?" she said lightly while keeping a tight hold on the smile on her face. She shouldn't have come, she realized too late. Her father was a superlative lawyer, and how could she have forgotten how adroitly he eventually obtained whatever information he desired?

"You know what I'm talking about," he said in his most stern I-am-your-father-and-don't-try-to-fool-me voice. "You lost weight as the result of having the flu, but this is ridiculous."

She knew she wouldn't be able to hold out against his persistence, and she looked at him with suddenly vulnerable eyes. "Don't, Dad," she pleaded. "Let it rest."

"Having problems at work?" he persisted.

Her tawny hair brushed her shoulders as she shook her head. "No." If it were only that!

A frown deepened as his gaze sharpened with realization. "No man is worth it, honey," he said softly.

Her lips quivered as she tried to force a smile. "That's what I keep saying, and one of these days I'll convince myself."

The waiter brought their cool drinks and she drank thirstily to ease the tightness closing her throat. Sensing that she could take no more questioning at that time, he changed the subject.

It was pleasant on the patio with a refreshing breeze coming off the golf links, and they elected to have lunch there before going in to change.

They enjoyed a hearty chef's salad and iced tea while chatting about interesting aspects of various cases they were involved in. The tension slowly receded, leaving Hannah more relaxed than she'd felt since her misguided decision to force Yale to follow her lead. For that was what it was, she realized with forlorn hindsight. She was so used to being in the driver's seat that she couldn't tolerate losing control. Unfortunately Yale was too strong a person to yield that command.

"By the way, I'm almost through with the paperwork turning over the adjacent property to Yale Upton. Do you remember him, my dear? You met him at the house and he had lunch at the club with us the next day."

The glow that the exercise had given to her complexion faded and Hannah quickly averted her face on hearing his name. As a result, she didn't see the considering expression in her father's eyes. She would never learn. She had thought herself safely finished with his probing.

"Mmm, yes," she agreed, using a deliberately vague tone.

"He's well into his expansion," her father continued while buttering a roll. "I expect big things from him, though I hope he isn't pushing himself too hard. He looked a little drawn when he was in the office yesterday."

Hannah had no concept of the hunger expressed in her eyes in her need for information about the subject of their conversation. He leaned back in his chair and obliged, his lids lowered so she couldn't see him evaluating her reaction.

"He's got an exceptionally astute business head. I can see him going as far as he allows his ambition to drive him. In fact, I'm thinking seriously of backing him financially in a small additional expansion he's contemplating. I've already told him I have some friends willing to join me in the venture."

That was accolade indeed, Hannah knew. Her father investigated such transactions thoroughly and had to be completely satisfied before committing himself, far less the money of friends.

Her mouth dropped in despondent lines. "I wish you well," she said in a small voice. Yale would be fully occupied now with little time for a woman in his life except in a very limited way. There'd be no time for the full-fledged affair he had hinted at, no time for anything as demanding as a marriage.

She placed the fork she was holding on the plate on finding her appetite had disappeared once more. She closed her eyes with a small sigh of acceptance. The reason behind the past weeks of agony could no longer be buried. She was in love with the man. That was why thoughts of marriage always intruded, and why she had backed away from his amorous advances in a futile hope that the delaying action would cause him to admit to a more lasting need for her than an affair.

She had gambled and lost. Where Yale was concerned she'd played the game all wrong. He had held all the cards from the very beginning. There was nothing left to do but hope the healing process started soon so she could again function as she had before he had come storming into her life.

"Do you want any dessert, dear?" her father asked, and she struggled to pull herself together on seeing the hovering waiter.

"I've had enough, thank you," she said, and pushed a hand wearily through her hair while her father signed the chit. "Next time I plan to redeem myself on the courts," she promised while placing a kiss on his cheek before leaving to change back into street clothes. "Give my love to Debbie. I assume she's behaving?"

"Naturally," he said dryly, and watched with troubled eyes as she strode to the lockers with the feline grace that was so like his.

Hannah was surprised the next morning to receive a call from Ted asking her if she felt like water skiing. "I haven't neglected you intentionally," he apologized. "It's just that I've been exceptionally busy."

"I hope that it was the right kind of busy," she mocked, and laughed on hearing his satisfied growl.

"Ivy and I planned a picnic and we've invited another couple and would like you to join us," he added. "If you have a friend you want to invite, bring him along. She's packed enough for an army."

"She's seen evidence of your appetite," she teased, not wanting to think of the man she wished she could ask. A vision of the way Yale had looked in his bathing suit on that memorable day spent in his sailboat rose before her, and she struggled against what it did to her pulse.

Later, with the spray wetting her face, she admitted she was glad she had accepted the invitation. Her lonely vigil by the phone had to cease. He was not about to call, and she had to accept that what they had shared was finished.

She maneuvered the single ski she was using across the wake, jumping the crest with carefree expertise. Seeing those on the boat applaud, she waved in acknowledgment.

The sun sparkled diamonds off the water and the accelerating speed made her feel suddenly free. A laugh bubbled up and she realized it was the first one in all too long a time. She reversed her hand on the tow rope as she executed a flawless turn. She was admittedly showing off, but having a grand time.

She was leaping off the high wave of a passing cruiser when she looked ahead and froze. A sailboat was moving off at an angle, and she recognized the graceful lines immediately. She bellyflopped into the water, carrying with her the picture of Yale at the tiller and a sleek brunette emerging from the cabin offering him a soda.

"Are you all right?" Anxious hands reached for her and

pulled her into the boat. "You just shot into the air and seemed to collapse. Are you sure you aren't hurt?"

She was too numb to hurt. Somehow she managed to laugh away their concern. "The rope slipped from my hand," she fabricated. "That will teach me to think I can fly!"

Shortly after they pulled up to a shelving beach and the women spread the picnic on several towels. Hannah assumed she was functioning normally; at least Bert, the date whom Ted had invited for her, didn't seem to notice anything odd in her behavior. She laughed, she nibbled at a section of sandwich, and drank too much of the cooled wine. She even let Bert place his arm around her when she saw the sailboat tack in their direction, as if needing him as a shield. She pulled away when the boat changed its course and raced rail down toward the far shore.

Her eyes followed the white sails until they were hidden by intervening boats. She sagged suddenly, feeling ages older since that carefree time when she had sat beside Yale, thrilling to the smoky glances that he kept sweeping over her, telling her of promises intended.

She was glad when they decided to call it a day and was deliberately vague when Bert pressed for a future date. She couldn't imagine sharing an evening with another man, of having other lips touch hers in a kiss. Time, she expected, would change that revulsion, but seeing Yale had reactivated raw nerves.

"I see you followed my advice," John said approvingly the following day when stopping by her office. "You don't look like a lost orphan any longer."

Hannah had to admit to feeling better. Her mirror had told her the weekend of outdoor activity had given color back to her face, and the exercise had rewarded her with a night of restful sleep.

"I thought I'd bring you up-to-date on the Upton case," he continued, occupying the chair by her desk and opening the folder she knew all too well.

"There's no need to," she protested quickly. "It's all yours now."

He gave a faint dismissive shrug before telling of the meeting he'd had with Yale. His glance slid over her questioningly, alerting Hannah of his curiosity over the real reason behind her turning down the case. After meeting the virile man, she was sure his guess was close to the truth, but thankfully he'd never know how complete had been her capitulation.

"I pulled two more potentials out of the morgue and set up appointments with him. He's pressing to get the right man for the job to free him for other things."

Only after John left did Hannah realize the tight hold she'd placed on herself. This had to stop, she warned herself grimly and mapped out a campaign to accomplish that feat.

She still drove herself relentlessly at work but was careful to curb her sharp tongue with her fellow employees. She forced herself to eat three meals a day and, realizing how the exercise had helped over the weekend, she now spent each evening jogging along the beach until she could barely pick up a foot. Sleep, as a result, was instantaneous when she dropped into bed.

The following weekend her father examined her with a qualified approval. Her outward appearance was much improved, but the inner glow that had been an integral part of her personality was missing. She looked sleek and finely honed, as if in condition to go the distance necessary to win a private race, but the joy wasn't there.

"You could have spared an old man's ego and not trounced me quite so badly," he mourned when they left the court.

They searched out their favorite table on the patio and she eyed him quizzically when he sneezed. "I have the feeling half of my luck came from the fact that you're coming down with a cold."

"You might be right," he admitted. "I'm counting on a good dose of sun and a sweat-out to help get me over it."

"It better," she grinned, "or Letta will be trying her home remedies on you." Letta guaranteed a cure for every ache or pain and over the years they'd found, surprisingly, quite a few worked.

"Debbie is into the latest in body-toning exercises and Letta's in her glory applying poultices and her special unguents for sore muscles." The two laughed, Hannah imagining her sister's disgust over the various medications. Letta could be quite formidable at any attempt to avoid her nursing care.

As was their custom, they shared the highlights of their week while eating their lunch. Hannah hadn't realized how she'd been waiting for the inevitable insertion of Yale's name into the conversation until it came. Was this the real reason she had called her father for another match on the tennis court, and not that she found a rematch necessary to redeem herself, the excuse she'd given him?

"We should finalize Upton's merger by the end of the week," he said, his gaze on his daughter while tasting the iced coffee. Hannah bent her concentration in searching for the shrimp in her salad and made no comment.

"We happened to meet in town the other day and we had lunch together. He had a charming woman with him, a Mrs. Dorminor, I believe."

The fork clattered to the plate and her hands slipped to her lap to hide their trembling. "Miss Dorminor," she corrected automatically.

He frowned momentarily. "No, I'm quite certain she was introduced as being married," he corrected. "And I'm certain one of the rings she was wearing was a wedding band. I take it you've met her?"

"I've only heard the name spoken," she admitted in a strained voice. She should have realized Yale's efficient Ms. Warwick would list all women under the Ms. title. Why had she assumed that the woman had been single?

"Are you certain you haven't met her?" her father persisted. "She seemed to know who I was talking about when your name came up. She's very attractive—tall, slender, dark hair cut short," he continued, as if to jog her memory.

Her memory was jogged all too painfully with pictures of the brunette in the restaurant and later in his sailboat. Could it be that they were all the same person, the Lois Dorminor whose dinner date was more important than his promise to her? All the knowledge proved, she admitted disconsolately, was that the frequency of their dates indicated she had been completely replaced in Yale's life.

She reached for her iced tea to ease the constriction in her throat. Long experience had taught her that her father's all-seeing eye missed little and already suspected he guessed some of the reason behind her performance the week before.

He leaned forward to capture her hand. "What is it, Hannah?" he asked earnestly. "What has happened to all that joie de vivre that always bubbled under the surface?"

His loving concern triggered an overlay of tears to rise and blur her vision. She knew what he meant. She'd usually viewed life with a ready laugh, but that ability had been sorely missing for the past few weeks. "Oh, Dad," she whispered, a half sob catching in her throat.

"It's Yale, isn't it?" he said gently. "I thought as much when I mentioned your name at that luncheon with him." He didn't elaborate further as his tender gaze took in her look of distress. "You've evidently been seeing each other. Can you tell me what happened, my dear?"

She looked at his dear face, remembering how as a child she had brought so many seemingly mammoth problems for him to solve, and the way they had always seemed to dissolve in the telling.

"There's nothing to tell, really," she began and, to her dismay, found herself relating the painful events: of a promised date being usurped by the same woman he'd met with Yale, of the kiss seen given in the restaurant, and the woman sharing his sailboat. "From your description, I guess they are all one and the same person," she concluded forlornly.

"A man is free to take out several women at the same time unless he's made some commitment," he reminded her pointedly.

Commitments! He'd demanded possession of her soul! "I thought he had," she confessed bitterly. "I was foolish to believe when he said he wouldn't tolerate any other man in my life that it worked both ways."

His lips pursed for a moment before he leaned back in the chair. "I would have thought the same of him. Are you certain you haven't misread the situation?"

Her eyes held rancor. "Your contact with him is through his business. I only hope he conducts it with more integrity than his private life."

"I've seldom guessed wrong on a person's character. But I realize that where affairs of the heart are concerned, people can act unpredictably." He gave a consoling pat to her hand.

The waiter came to ask if they wanted dessert and his interruption brought an end to the painful subject, for which Hannah was thankful. She hadn't expected her father to solve her problem, but just sharing it with him somehow lifted some of the heaviness from her heart.

"Do we have a tennis date next week?" he asked when he signed the bill.

"I'll call later this week," she promised. She'd leave the week open for now. It was time to get back into the mainstream and accept some of the offers of dates that she'd been ignoring. She was tired of the lurch to her heart that came whenever the phone rang, and the resulting ache when the deep purr wasn't heard.

Eyes followed them as they walked together to the lockers, a tall handsome couple, a matching gold with sun-streaked hair and long graceful strides.

"Bear up, my dear. It's always darkest before dawn, and with that worn, but frequently true, platitude I'll leave you," he said, placing a consoling kiss on her cheek.

An attractive woman called his name and he turned to her with a welcoming smile. Hannah continued on to change, wondering if she was one of the long succession of women who had tried unsuccessfully to persuade her father he could love someone else as much as he had his wife. She hoped for his sake he could find an adequate replacement only because she wished away his inner loneliness. She then thought of Yale and prayed that someone would come to replace him, even while knowing it was a wasted wish.

She spent her time while driving home going over a mental list of men friends she could call to let them know she was ready to circulate again. She ticked them off one by one and knew with a sinking heart that there were none who could even begin to help her in the healing. How had she ever been able to enjoy their companionship? In comparison to one particularly vibrant man's personality, they paled into nothingness.

CHAPTER TEN

Hannah tapped her pen absently on the desk top as she stared thoughtfully out her office window. The next day would end another week and she played over the past few evenings, wondering if it was worth the expenditure of energy to continue with her plan.

On arriving home after her confession time with her father, she'd put her decision to work and had called several of the more appealing men on her list. Their instant response had been heartwarming to her bruised self-image. She'd determinedly gone out the following nights and, until the phone call she'd just received, had a date for this one also. He'd apologized profusely, saying a rush order made it imperative that he work late, and how soon could he see her again. She was now left with the decision whether she should call someone else, and gave a sigh, realizing it would take more of an effort than she felt like expending.

The week, she admitted resignedly, had been a dismal failure. The men were charming, the places they took her were interesting. But no matter how hard she tried to infuse some warmth into the end of the evenings, the kisses had been a trial to endure. Each one had left her shaken as if she had been a traitor, and she'd found herself stumbling to the bathroom to scrub her mouth with childish thoroughness.

She welcomed the ring of the telephone as a reason to end her sense of futility. Still, she intended to continue the course she was on until her life once again fell into place.

"Miss Hannah?" It was Letta, her father's housekeeper, and she came immediately to attention.

"What is it?" she asked in alarm. "Is anything wrong?" Letta had never called at the office before and she couldn't quell the rising apprehension.

"Nothing, really, Miss Hannah," the woman replied. "It's just your father . . . Well, you know how stubborn he is! I know he's got a temperature and he won't take care of himself. Even now he's working in the study when he should be in bed. He won't take any of my medicines to help him, and I thought you could talk some sense into him."

"I'll be right over," she promised, already sweeping the files she was working on into a drawer. If Letta took the time to call, she must really be worried. She was recalling the cold he was fighting that weekend, and berated herself for not at least phoning to check how he was doing. The flu she'd suffered with had almost developed into pneumonia. He was older and would be more susceptible.

By the time she reached the house, she had worked herself into a fine steam, already visualizing her father in the hospital with an oxygen tent and fluid dripping into his veins. She loved him devotedly, and the reminder of the frailty of life hit her hard.

"How is he?" she asked breathlessly after running up the steps. The fact that Letta was waiting for her seemed ominous. Had he taken a turn for the worse?

"He's still in the library," she said darkly. "I made some fresh tea from my special herbs and I'll bring it in. Make sure he drinks it, you hear?"

She quickly agreed while striding hurriedly to the library. When he looked up from the desk he was working at and smiled in pleased surprise, she leaned against the frame and laughed weakly. And here she'd had him at death's door!

She should have remembered Letta, when acting the nurse, was formidable about any refusal of her treatments and ministrations. She dropped into the chair by the desk and soon had her father laughing with her when she related the near panic Letta's call had caused.

"I'm sorry she had you racing out here," he said, and reached for an outsize tissue he used when suffering from a cold. "But I admit the unexpected visit is a pleasure."

He blew his nose and Hannah examined him carefully. Letta had been right in one account. He was in the worst stage of the virus. His face was flushed and his eyes watery, and his voice had a harsh rasp to it. He was wearing the handsome bathrobe she'd given him for Christmas over his pajamas.

"Why aren't you in bed?" she asked in exasperation.

"I've been there for the past two days," he informed her. "And before you join Letta and scold me, I'll agree to go back there as soon as I finish these papers. They have to be filed tomorrow. I had them sent over so I could get them ready for the proper signatures."

"With the notoriously slow way that courts move, did you have to risk getting pneumonia?" she asked, her irritation showing. "Another day wouldn't make any difference."

"You don't understand filing deadlines," he said dismissively. "I admit bed will feel good after I get these to him for his signature."

"Don't tell me you intend to deliver them also!" she cried in alarm. "Tell me where they have to go and I'll take them."

He looked at her for a long minute, and she licked suddenly dry lips, already sensing what he was about to say.

"Yale promised he'd get them to the courthouse first thing in the morning," he said slowly.

"No!" The protest was a bare whisper.

"I just got off the phone with him," he said hurriedly before she could say more. "I told him I'd get them to him right away. I thought Deborah was home and I was going to ask her, but Letta informed me she'd called to say she was going on to dinner with a bunch of friends."

Hannah shook her head wordlessly. Knowing her story, how could he think to ask her to go to Yale's house . . . to face his certain rejection.

"We had an interesting conversation," he continued, his eyes returning to the papers, as if unaware of her consternation. "I was interested in a clarification on an impression I was left with during that lunch I had with him." He looked up suddenly and impaled his daughter with sharp, amber eyes. "Did you know that Lois Dorminor is his cousin?"

"Oh, dear God!" The whispered cry escaped as a sigh of utter desolation. What had her jealousy-fed mind done!

He slid the papers he was working on into a manila envelope and handed it to her. "I think he rates an apology of sorts, don't you?" he said gently.

"Oh, Dad! How can I!" she wailed.

"You're an intelligent woman. You'll find a way," he said firmly. His expression softened on seeing her quail at the thought. "Let me tell you something, my dear. I had twenty-five of the most wonderful years of my life with your mother. To my everlasting regret I know I could have had three more if I hadn't been so stubborn in believing I had to wait until I was in the position to give her the things she deserved. Pride can be a very cold bedfellow."

The message was clear and Hannah reached for the envelope with trembling fingers. Already she had wasted a month out of her life without being in his arms. A deep love for her understanding parent flooded her.

"Pray for me," she whispered huskily as she kissed him. She hurried by a surprised Letta, almost upsetting the tray holding a steaming cup of tea.

"Drink it all, love," she called gaily over her shoulder. "I'll keep you posted!"

Her car seemed instinctively to know the way to Yale's house. She'd never been there, but he'd given his address during one of their shared exchanges. Not until she pulled into the driveway and saw the pristine white Roman pillared entrance did the first misgivings hit her. Her hands clutched the steering wheel with white-knuckled intensity. What in the world was she doing here? She could already see his gray eyes darken in anger, or, even worse, silver in cool indifference. How did she ever think she could effect a reconciliation?

She reached to turn on the ignition and make her escape when her gaze fell on the manila envelope. She'd left her father flying on a cloud of unreasonable hope, but the fact remained she had promised him to deliver the important documents. She drew in a long, steadying breath and opened the car door. Surely a maid at least came along with such a pretentious house. She'd simply hand the envelope to the person . . . and run.

"Will you please give this to Mr. Upton?" she said hurriedly when a somber-dressed, gray-haired man opened the door to her ring.

"This way, miss," he said, ushering her in. "Mr. Upton is waiting for you in his study."

Hannah obeyed with a sense of inevitability. He was expecting her sister, of course, and followed him reluctantly to her fate. The entrance, she noted vaguely, was beautiful in its purity. It was built in the era when marble was used with a lavish hand, and the floors and walls glistened white. It was a perfect background for the graceful sweep of stairs, its black, intricate iron-lace bannister standing out in exquisite detail. She'd been in many of the homes in Palm Beach, but none could surpass the beauty of the architectural detail in this foyer.

"Mr. Upton," the houseman said formally as he opened a handsomely paneled door.

She was barely aware of the door closing behind her. Yale was at his desk, busily writing on one of the papers littering its top.

His head remained bent and he frowned slightly at the interruption. "Be with you in a second," he murmured, not permitting any intrusion into his concentration.

He could take all the time he wanted to, she admitted as her heart beat a traitorous tattoo. She examined him with hungry eyes that busily imprinted his image on her heart. Her fingers twitched with memories of how his crisp black hair had felt under their stroking, how comfortably her head had fit on that broad shoulder. Her gaze slid to the strong hand with the supple fingers clasping the pen and her flesh burned recalling the glories it had performed on her body.

She tore her gaze away to slide back to his face. It looked harsher than she had remembered. There were new hollows and the lines grooving his mouth were deeper. The pressure from expanding his business was leaving its mark. Still, the new severity only accented his aggressive features with an additional attractiveness. His was a face no one could forget, and the fact was driven home with a new clarity.

He dropped his pen finally and looked up. Hannah was momentarily scorched by the fire that leapt in his eyes, only to be promptly veiled as he rose slowly from his seat.

"Hannah," he said coolly, "this is a surprise."

The reserve in his voice had her doubting what she had thought she'd seen and the conflict left her suddenly unable to speak until she cleared her throat.

"I believe Dad gave you the necessary instructions about signing these and where to take them in the morning."

He merely nodded and she shifted uncomfortably under his unwavering gaze.

"My sister was supposed to bring them but she had a date, and since I was there, I was delegated. Dad's suffering from a miserable cold, so I wouldn't allow him to do it himself. You do realize he got out of a sick bed to get these ready for you!" She knew she was babbling on like a fool, but somehow she couldn't stop.

"I'm sorry. I knew he had a cold, but I didn't know it was that severe."

"Yes . . . well . . ." She looked helplessly around, her mind curiously devoid of anything further to say. If only he didn't keep staring at her from shuttered eyes that gave her no hint of what he was thinking!

He put his hand out for the envelope and she realized with a start that she still held it clutched to her. She had remained by the door, as if the distance would keep her out of his orbit and give her some sort of protection. She now moved jerkily to the desk and handed the envelope to him.

Why didn't he say something? she agonized as she stared at him. Anything. Just one word of encouragement. She had come to ask his forgiveness in doubting him, to tell him he had her complete trust as he'd demanded, but his tightly controlled features gave her no opening.

Her lashes fluttered down in helpless resignation. "I'm sorry to have bothered you. I know you're busy."

She turned away and moved stiffly in retreat. Just a few more steps, she thought despairingly, and she'd be out of his life and she accepted with a painful finality that she had no one to blame but herself.

No! The protest rose bitingly in her. She had to make one last confession. She owed it to him. Perhaps then he'd have kinder memories of her, could find it in him to forgive the foolish creature he'd once desired.

She paused at the door, her hand resting on the knob. She half-turned, but found it impossible to look at him, and fastened her gaze blindly at the carpet so she wouldn't have to see his implacable expression.

"One thing more before I go," she said in a strained voice. "I owe you an apology. You asked for trust and I acted the fool. I didn't know Lois Dorminor was your cousin. I only knew you were canceling our date in order to go out with her. Of course, a relative had preference over me." She raised her face to stretch her neck in an attempt to ease the rawness burning her throat. "The next day I saw you in Bentley's, kissing a stunning woman and that weekend you were sailing with her." She squeezed her eyes shut against remembered pain. "I thought you were using the double standard. It was all right for you to date others even while you insisted I stop. And my pride wouldn't allow me to tolerate that."

She waited a fraction of time for some response. Hearing nothing, she tugged at the door. She was halfway across the marble foyer before she was pulled to a stop.

"Hannah!" His hands fastened on her shoulders and she was turned roughly to face him. She'd seen his anger before, but it was nothing to the fury she was now witnessing. "Do you mean you've put me through these weeks of hell just because you didn't have the sense to ask about what you assumed? My God, woman, I could shake you until you couldn't use that stupid head any longer!"

He proceeded to show what he meant, until with a groan she was crushed in his arms with his mouth fastened on hers. She tasted his anger, his frustration, and finally with a slight gentling, his hunger.

Her mouth moved under his, telling him of her matching longing, of the emptiness that had been endured. It had been so long, and she had thought she'd never feel that wonderful sensuous exploration again! The loneliness, the agony she'd suffered through disappeared into nothingness. There was only the glory of being in his arms, of being pressed against the rock-hard length of him and slowly drowning in the rapture only his kisses could evoke.

With great reluctance his mouth released hers. She buried her face in the warmth of his neck, breathing deeply of the muskiness that was his alone. His cheek rested on her hair as his hands traced memory trips over her rib cage and down her back until they cupped her firm bottom to pull her into the cradle of his thighs.

She arched into him with surging passion on feeling his need. It had been so long . . . so long . . .

Little sounds of protest rose in her throat when he moved to permit space between them. "Not here, not in the hall," he muttered with evident reluctance. He led her back to his study, his arm keeping her tucked against his side.

The door was closed behind them and she was again swept into his arms. It was pure delight; the kisses held no reservation as his mouth, his tongue took possession in a domination that was a submission. Her blouse was pulled free of her skirt and his hands explored with a thoroughness as if needing to reaffirm memories. She became a vessel yearning for him to drink his fill, and she clung to him, her limbs weakened by the force of her desire.

He finally tore his mouth away and crushed her back in his arms. His heart thundered against her breast, and she wondered if he was as vibrantly aware of her answering beat. But this wasn't what she wanted. She needed his lips on hers, his hands tracing her body, his complete possession. She pressed sinuously against him and moaned with her need as she raised her face expectantly to his.

"Hush, sweet heart," he said thickly. "Don't move, please! Give me time to get a handle on myself. We have to talk first before we go any further."

She saw no need to talk. They were doing all the communicating necessary, but she stilled her movements as requested, realizing with a supreme joy that the effect she had on him equaled what he triggered in her. When their racing hearts slowly returned to normal, and the heat flushing their bodies cooled, he placed a chaste kiss on her forehead and released his hold.

"I have a strong need for a drink. Join me?" he asked, moving to an unobtrusive bar fitted into the bookshelves lining one wall.

He carefully selected a chair across from her after handing her the glass, as if well aware that any touching would end his resolve to talk. "I want to explain about Lois," he began.

"It isn't necessary," she interrupted. After their passionate exchange, the woman had receded into a nonentity.

"Hush and listen," he insisted firmly. "You already made the issue important and I don't want it to rise up and haunt us again. Lois is my cousin through my father's sister. Her father was an engineer and his life has been spent in the hinterland of any nation that decided they needed roads built to open the back country. As soon as

Lois was old enough, she was sent to boarding schools, her mother deciding her place was by her husband. My parents sort of adopted her and she became the little sister that I never had."

He paused to sip his scotch, his expression showing his regression into memories. "She was a cute kid and I guess I kind of spoiled her. Anyway, I found it fun acting the big brother, helping her solve her problems and riding herd on her boyfriends. With her parents away most of the time, I guess it was only natural for her to look to me as a substitute."

He rubbed the back of his neck and gave a wry grimace. "Well, the little girl grew up and four years ago got married and went to California to live. She'd always been a little immature emotionally, so when she'd call whenever she had a problem, I'd let her talk it out as had been her habit, hoping with time she'd learn to cope. The marriage started to get rockier a few months ago and her calls became more frequent. I let her unburden herself, hoping by talking she'd work it all out, but last month she said she'd had it and was flying back with her son."

Hannah felt terrible. She'd been the fool again, allowing her jealousy to take over. He had asked for trust, and she'd given him suspicion. He'd already told her how essential it was to him, but she'd been too wrapped up in her self-induced misery to listen and unwittingly let her action tear apart the tender fabric of their budding relationship.

She met his stare, letting her eyes beg for forgiveness. "We all have had some growing up to do," she admitted in a low voice.

The corners of his eyes crinkled in the beginning of a smile. "I think we have a long-delayed date for dinner. Shall I pick you up at seven?" He was finished with the subject. He'd given his story and considered her intelligent enough to fill in the gaps.

She could only nod her head because of the constriction in her throat. His smoky eyes moved over her and she quivered in response. Tonight, she knew breathlessly, tonight they'd wipe out the intervening hurtful weeks, burying them under their tomorrows.

He moved to the bar to pour a refill. "And by the way," he said over his shoulder, "that call you heard at the office was to tell me she'd arrived safely. I wanted her to come to dinner with us. I thought being a woman, she'd relate more to you and you'd be in a better position to help her through the first difficult days."

Hannah closed her eyes in pain. Oh, yes, she'd acted the fool! Without the overlay of jealousy, she could see in retrospect how that kiss in the restaurant had held compassion, and how he'd have used the ride in his boat in an attempt to lighten her spirits.

Her eyes flew open on hearing the door being opened. "There you are, Yale! Don't you think you've hidden long enough in this room? It's time to relax before freshening for dinner." The willowy brunette ran lightly to Yale and planted a kiss on his cheek, and Hannah struggled against the instant resentment on seeing her easy familiarity.

So, she was meeting Lois Dorminor at last! Even as she fought it, the picture rose of her using his affection as an excuse to rest in his arms. Could any woman, even a cousin help falling in love with him? Didn't he see why her marriage was doomed to failure? A chill settled around her heart as her emotions began their retreat.

Yale turned her to face Hannah. "Lois, I want you to meet Hannah Blake." He draped his arm casually across her shoulders as he smiled across the room. "Hannah, my cousin Lois."

Hannah rose slowly to her feet. "How do you do," she said coolly. God, how was she going to act natural when she wanted to dash across the room and tear his arm from contact with the woman!

"Unca Yay, Unca Yay!" A little fireball of energy dressed adorably in miniature trousers, shirt, and tie dashed across the room. Yale bent down immediately to catch him and swoop him up in the air amid squeals of delight.

"And this," he said, sitting the little boy on his shoulder, "is Jay."

Two heads with the same black hair turned to her, and she met identical sets of smoky gray eyes. And she swayed as the blood drained from her face.

CHAPTER ELEVEN

Hannah sank into the chair and groped blindly for her drink, vaguely aware of Lois's voice threading through the ringing in her ears.

"What do you think of my son?" she asked proudly. "Jay, say how do you do to the lady."

Yale placed the boy on the floor so he could obey instructions. He stayed where he was as Jay came politely forward. The smile had left his face and Hannah sensed him retreating as she had.

Don't read me so quickly! she cried in silent anguish. *Give me time to get over the shock and unfreeze my brain!*

She had an above-average intelligence. Why did it always go into hibernation and allow her emotions to take over where Yale was concerned! She was desperately aware that she never had more need to regain control over her senses. The torn fabric of what was special between them had been sewn together with gossamer threads. If it tore apart again before she could strengthen the binding, she knew she was lost forever.

The small chubby hand touched hers and she forced a

smile to wooden lips. On closer inspection his features were nothing like Yale's. Only the hair. Only the eyes. "Did Uncle Yale give you a big ride?" she asked with appropriate interest.

"Unca Yay make airplane!" He spread his arms out and, making motor noises, he zoomed back to the tall man, there to wrap his arms around a muscular leg and laugh in glee as he looked for approval for his masterful act.

"He adores Yale," Lois said unnecessarily. "We're lucky to have him and to be able to stay here until I straighten out my life."

She was living in this house with him! The fact came like one more hammer blow. She rose on shaking legs. "It was nice meeting you," she said in a voice she didn't recognize. "But I have to go now. Don't forget to sign those papers, Yale, and get them early to the courthouse." She was babbling again. The only way to stop was to leave, and quickly.

Yale walked with her in silence to the door and across the marble foyer. Her heels clicked like peals of doom. *Say something! Do something!* she wanted to scream, but by the time they reached the outer door, she knew that once again he was leaving it up to her to make the first move. He'd forced the issue during their early days, but now she had to show she'd reached her maturity.

Her head had cleared somewhat and she could again reason. For heaven's sake, hadn't she studied about heredity and genes! After all, he and Lois were related. There was no call to have jumped to such a horrendous conclusion with her jealous-sick mind.

When he reached for the doorknob, she stepped in front of him. Her hands went to his shoulders and she raised on tiptoe to place a light kiss on his lips. "You have an adorable nephew, Yale . . . and a very attractive cousin. And I'll be ready at seven."

He nodded slowly and she hurried down the steps to her car. She glanced back at the house before driving away and saw his dark outline in the doorway as he waited to see her off. She gave what she hoped was a cheerful beep on the horn in farewell, but she was left with the image of the frowning thoughtfulness expressed on his face after her kiss.

What had she done? she fretted, shaking. She wasn't fooling herself that he hadn't noticed her shock on seeing Jay, and with his uncanny ability to crawl into her mind guessed at the reason behind it. Anger rose in her, and disgust. If she permitted her uncalled-for jealous reaction to drive him away again, she had no one to blame but herself. She loved the man, and it was time for her to stop acting the immature nitwit. If she ever behaved in a similar fashion at work, she'd not only lose the respect of her coworkers but would be out of a job. Before matching clients and a position, she'd always researched their weak points as much as the positive ones. As a result, she was proud of the string of successful matches she'd made. It would be smart tactics to consider using that same business strategy with Yale. It could well be her most challenging assignment.

She didn't have time for the long leisurely bath she'd prefer, but when she stepped out of the shower she rubbed a seductively scented oil over her still wet body before drying herself. As a result, a fine layer of perfume covered her soft, silky skin.

She had already mentally gone through her wardrobe and had decided upon a pale beige dress that closely matched her skin tones. It was made from a fine see-through lacy knit material. She had seen similar ones worn without bras, but she admitted a shyness about acting that deliberate, and topped the half slip with a mini-bra that she was quite unaware was more provoking for partially hiding the treasures beneath.

She spent careful minutes with her makeup, stroking on the blusher and outlining her lids with black kohl that gave added excitement to her amber eyes. The low-scooped neckline demanded a necklace and she selected a single strand of fine pearls. Her tanned legs didn't need stockings, she decided, so she slipped into white high-heeled strappy sandals.

He was always punctual, she remembered, and was waiting breathlessly for him five minutes before the hour. Her campaign was simple. She had to rebuild the delicate mood that they had shared before she'd shattered it after the introduction of his cousin and her son. At this point the only weapon she was certain of was the physical one neither of them could deny. She'd start with that and let her instincts take it from there. Once on a firmer footing she'd somehow contrive to reaffirm her vow of trust. He'd been deeply scarred by a jealous mother; it was up to her to show it was possible to give love untainted by that soul-tearing emotion. He hadn't asked for love, only a commitment, but she had long ago accepted that that was what she had to offer. If he couldn't reciprocate that love, she'd accept him at whatever bittersweet level he'd want to conduct the affair. The past month had proven she couldn't live without him. She was his as long as he wanted her.

The buzzer alerted her to his arrival and after pressing the release she recalled with a twinge of sadness for that initially confusing but happy time when he had the freedom of her key. Would she be able to wipe the slate clean and be given a second chance?

Her hands clasped tight in sudden anxiety on hearing the elevator stop, and she resolutely cleared her mind.

She'd never permit herself to face a client with a negative attitude, and much rode on this evening with Yale.

She swung the door open for him. He stood ravishingly handsome, dressed in a checked two-tone brown jacket and cream-colored slacks. She gave him a bright smile in greeting and didn't permit it to falter when he didn't sweep her into his arms as he once had.

"I have your drink ready," she said, moving to the tray holding the glasses. "I thought we'd have one before we went out. That is, if we have time?" She arched an eyebrow in question as she glanced over her shoulder, pausing long enough so he had a full view of the way the dress accented her slender back and the fetching firm bottom. *Do you remember how you'd curve your hands here, snuggling me close so I'd flame with awareness of your desire?*

Her hands trembled momentarily before reaching for the crystal glasses. "I hope it's mixed right," she said, handing him one while sipping from the other.

She moved with gliding grace to the sofa and her lashes dropped quickly to hide the disappointment when he chose a chair across from her. *Think positive,* she reminded herself bracingly, and gave a feline stretch, extending her long slim legs with their sexy shoes for his inspection.

She watched his eyes make their inventory and hid her smile by taking another taste of her drink. A new excitement was tripping through her. She'd never played this role before, had never had to, but she could see why some women got their thrills from being the seducer. By the time the evening was over, she intended to have successfully eroded through the reserve he still wore as a shield. She had to. She could think of no other way to prove her trust.

She questioned with interest how his expansion was going, and was thankful he made no question of why John had replaced her, when he said he thought he'd found the ideal man to run the enlarged plant. Unconsciously her hand slid under the heavy fall of hair and lifted it from her neck. It was a habit she had to permit a refreshing cooling. Her pulse leaped erratically on catching flame momentarily behind the smoke. *Are you remembering how you loved to run your hands through it, burying your face in the silken strands before letting it filter through your fingers?*

She jumped up suddenly and moved to the tray. "Can I interest you in another?" she asked. Emotion made her voice sound thin. She was caught in her own web. They'd better finish quickly and go. He'd have to find out about her trust in some other way. She couldn't play the temptress, the seductress . . .

"You're a Lorelei," he said from behind her, and she quivered over how he again had meshed his thoughts with hers.

His arms wrapped around her, drawing her close to him. His face remained buried in her hair for long minutes while his hands searched for and cupped the weight of her breasts. He turned her around slowly until she faced him and her face lifted for the kiss denied her since his arrival. She was already melting in anticipation, with tiny tendrils of excitement alerting her nerve paths of the rapture soon to be felt.

"This is what you want, isn't it?" he asked, and her eyes widened in confusion in seeing the cynical expression on his face before his mouth came down hard on hers. There was no tenderness, no gentleness, only a male need for satisfaction. She wanted to protest in surprise, but her traitorous body had already found and fitted her soft curves against the appropriate muscular angles of his body. Something was wrong, but all thought melted into mist as she responded with an ardor he'd expertly programed in her, beginning with his first kiss.

"If we keep this up, we won't make that reservation,"

he warned grimly. She shivered slightly on seeing the fires burn through the smoke. But where was the tender smile, the gentle stroking fingers?

"Yale?" It was a bewildered plea.

The harsh angles of his face softened a fraction, but it was all she needed. Her arms were around his neck, pulling his head down. "Reservations were made to be broken," she breathed against his lips.

They were soon in her bed, their clothes thrown on a chair. His hands sought all her tender areas, playing on their known response, but even when in the delirium of their blending rhythm, she sensed something lacking. His expertise was just as commanding, but she felt instinctively as if a small part of him were kept withdrawn. Only then did she realize the complete giving they had once shared, and she strove with every movement, every searching, urging caress to show that with her nothing had changed from before. She was his completely—heart, mind, body, and soul. Then his thrusts were deeper and faster, and all the half formed and vague questions slithered away as she rode with him into that outer space where they touched briefly on their private star.

"Ah, sweet heart, there's no one like you," he admitted with a kiss before withdrawing from her.

She smiled drowsily at him. "I'm sorry I don't have the same background for comparison, but something tells me I've a winner!"

He laughed warmly. "Remember that," he said, placing a teasing kiss on the tip of her nose before pulling her close so their bodies were in full contact.

She must have been wrong, she reasoned sleepily while snuggling closer. Surely his response was warm enough now.

The coolness along her side woke Hannah and she opened her eyes to see Yale sitting on the edge of the bed.

"I don't know about you, but I'm starved," he announced. "I know a place that stays open late and serves great barbecued ribs. Are you on?"

A short time later she was grinning at him while nibbling at the succulent ribs. "I'm glad this is a place where I can pick them up in my fingers," she commented. The glamorous dress had done its job very adequately, she had conceded glowingly when pulling on jeans and a scarlet blouse. While she might have enjoyed an evening dancing with him, his arms had been put to better use. And his kisses. And his body.

Her smile deepened, causing an eyebrow to raise in question. "I wonder what's behind that Mephistophelean smile," he probed.

"I was wondering how to lure you back to my apartment and not frighten you away," she said with an audacious leer.

He threw his head back with a roar of laughter. She stared mesmerized at the bronze column of his throat and wondered what he'd think if she'd give in to the overpowering desire to lean forward and place a kiss there.

His laugh stopped and she stared aghast at the barbecue sauce staining his throat. Had she in her euphoria done that? She reached with trembling hand to wipe it away with her napkin.

"If you're not careful," he advised in a husky voice when she finished, "you won't be given time to finish eating."

She carefully selected another rib before giving him an impudent grin. "Then I guess we better hurry up and eat. It wouldn't do for you to get faint from hunger."

"Hannah!" he warned, and they shared wide smiles as they finished their platters and drained the beer.

Whatever lingering questions Hannah might have had about any restraint on Yale's part disappeared under the delight of the rest of the evening. They were again enjoying the easy rapport they'd experienced before, the give and take that was quite separate from the sensual rapture they shared while in bed.

"I'm going to be working on a tight schedule for the next month," he warned when they started on the strawberry-rhubarb pie, a specialty of the house.

"Your father has performed miracles in pushing through the paperwork, and Bryan has obligingly let me start some necessary renovation on the building for the heavy machinery that will be coming shortly."

"Does that mean I won't see very much of you?" She couldn't hide the forlorn tone from invading the question.

His hand captured hers on the table top. "You'll see me every free minute I can spare," he said. "I'm just alerting you so you know that if I don't call, or if several days pass without seeing you, it's because I'm tied up with pressing problems that have to be resolved. I have to get those new presses going as fast as I can. I've some contracts with deadlines I have to meet, so I can pay for all this expansion. Once things get rolling, I can place it all in my new supervisor's hands. That's what I'm hiring him for. You do understand, don't you?"

"Of course," she smiled reassuringly, thrilled that he needed her understanding. A day without him now would be so very different from the empty bleakness of the past weeks when there'd been no hope of ever seeing him again.

They left then and drove back to her apartment. "You see, you don't have to resort to any tactics to get me back here," he said meaningfully when, after locking the door behind them, he gathered her in his arms. His gaze was hooded as it traveled over her face, taking in the slumbering invitation in her amber eyes, the promise of softening lips. She was crushed to his chest in a painful hold that she reveled in when sensing his urgency. "Don't you ever dare repeat what you pulled these past weeks, Hannah Blake, or I promise you won't sit for a week!" he threatened in a fierce voice. "I refuse to go through that hell again."

"If it will make you feel any better, I was there too!" she confessed, her mouth trailing small kisses along his throat and over the slight roughness of his jaw. She knew what they were doing to him—wasn't she crushed tight against his wonderful body? But he'd given her the perfect opening she'd sought, and now was the time to lay bare her soul as she had planned before she melted into him and lost all thread of thought.

But how did one go about confessing a love when the man had given no indication he wanted that deep a commitment between them? How could she say "I love you, Yale"?

"I love you, Yale." She buried her forehead against his neck to hide her flaming cheeks. Had she really said that aloud? His hands had stilled and she knew he'd heard her. Oh, Lord, why did she have to start that way! Quickly, before she lost courage, she hastened on with her planned confession. "I know you're not interested in that, but I have to tell you so you can understand something about why I acted as I did. I've never been in love before, at least nothing as consuming as what I feel now, and I wasn't prepared for all the auxiliary spinoffs, like making love so soon. I never gave a key to anyone before." She drew in a deep breath, knowing she was rambling again. "But the bad part was being jealous. I've never experienced it before, and was unprepared for how devastating it could be. I didn't know how to handle my mixed-up emotions and I foolishly let it come between us. But I promise I've learned my lesson and won't let it happen again."

She raised her head and looked at him beseechingly. "You have no idea how horrible it is to be consumed with such uncontrollable doubts."

"Don't I?" he said, a wry smile curling his lips. "Why do you think I wanted you to stop all other dating? I felt a pompous fool demanding that of you after knowing me for such a short time. You had every right to toss me out on my ear. But I couldn't help myself. I saw red—or green, if you like—whenever I thought of you being with any other man."

"Oh, Yale!" Her eyes glowed with her love.

He took her waiting lips, effectively stopping further conversation. This time the kiss began with the gentleness that had been missing before. Then her senses, which were always willing, kindled to his torch and were soon ablaze with a rapturous fire.

It was only later, after he placed last lingering kisses on her breasts before pulling the covers over her and getting dressed, that she realized he had said nothing about a reciprocated love.

She fought the ache building in her on hearing the door close behind him. Hadn't she said that she'd accept this affair at any level he chose? And now the test had started.

With a muffled cry she buried her face in the pillow that had so recently held his head, drawing in deep breaths of his lingering musky scent. She fell asleep, finally, the pillow clasped in her arms.

CHAPTER TWELVE

"I want to tell you about the Upton case," John said, coming into Hannah's office and perching his hip on the edge of her desk. "He hired a Boris Winthrop. His job had terminated three months ago, so he was able to take a room in town and starting today will be sitting in with Mr. Upton to find out what's wanted. He's quite excited. It's not always one finds a job where one's imprint can be placed from the beginning."

Hannah listened with pretended interest. It wouldn't do to let him know that she already had all that information, and more, from the source. "Mr. Dunn will be happy that you brought it so quickly to a successful conclusion."

"Well, you did most of the groundwork," he admitted magnanimously.

The way he quirked an eye at her warned her that he was still intrigued over why she'd turned the case over to him, but she had no intention of filling him in even though the original reason was no longer valid. A glow warmed her face as she recalled how thoroughly that reason had been negated the night before.

"I see you've solved the problem with the boyfriend," he said knowingly on seeing her softened expression.

She looked at him startled. Lord, how had he found out about Yale!

"Whoever he is, he must be some man," he continued with an exaggerated leer. "Well, good luck, kiddo. As they say, it's love that makes the world go around." He placed a brotherly pat on her shoulder and gave a thumbs-up sign as he departed.

Yes, she admitted, conscious of the happiness welling in her, it was love that made *her* world go around. With that satisfying admission, she turned to the folders on her desk. Gone was the despairing need to bury herself in her work, and she was surprised to see just as much could be accomplished without the past desperate dedication.

Yale called after lunch to inform her he wouldn't see her for dinner that night but would come later. He arrived close to ten and they enjoyed a slow leisurely love time. She was aware of the tired lines around his eyes so, while disappointed, she wasn't surprised when he called the following day to say he'd be working late and wouldn't see her that night.

She voiced her concern on Wednesday when he arrived late and she saw the weariness was more pronounced. "Isn't your new man any help?" she asked, wondering if his choice was, after all, unequal to the requirements.

"I'm working the pants off him," Yale admitted. "There's just a thousand and one other details that only I can handle at this point. I'm always fighting delays and breakdowns in lines of communication. It's like fighting the clock while working a giant jigsaw. If one piece isn't in place on time, the next one can't be added."

She mixed his scotch on the rocks with a dash of water the way he liked it and brought it to him. He took an appreciative sip before patting the cushion beside him on the sofa. She cuddled next to him in companionable silence until he finished his drink, sensing he needed the rest to regroup himself.

"I missed you last night," she said softly. "And I'd have missed you twice as much tonight, but you should have stayed home and gone to bed."

"You're right, but I had to come," he confessed as he drew her close to place a kiss on her temple. "I find one day without seeing you is all I can take."

She let the words flow through her, savoring the interpretation they could be given. Perhaps one day, when the pressure of the expansion was behind him, he would have time to analyze the extent of his attraction to her and come up with the answer she longed to hear. Meanwhile she was content to accept each day, one at a time, as long as he was part of them.

Wrapping a towel around her after showering, she stepped into the bedroom only to pause in the doorway, a rueful smile forming. Yale had stripped before stretching on the bed when she'd gone to the bathroom and he was now fast asleep. She visually possessed him for long minutes, drinking in the beauty of his perfectly formed body, before joining him in bed and pulling up the covers. She didn't have the heart to awaken him, but on some unconscious level he must have sensed her near him, and his arm came out to pull her close.

The alarm went off and Hannah found herself curved along the long line of Yale's back. She felt him stiffen slightly on awakening as he assimilated where he was. He turned slightly, lifting his head to see the time.

"Poor planning, love," he grimaced. "You should have set the alarm earlier." He then twirled rapidly while throwing the light sheet back on finishing his turn. Before she could move, he leaned over her, his body imprinted on hers. "It's a case of breakfast or . . . which do you choose?"

"That's a big decision to make so early in the morning," she returned solemnly, her mouth pursed in thought. Her palms rubbed over his arms, bridging her as she lay trapped under him.

"Perhaps this will aid the thought process," he said helpfully as his thigh pressed between hers.

"Oh, my, yes, that does help!" she agreed, her eyes glowing with her answer. Her hands buried in his sleep-tousled hair, pulling him down to her waiting mouth and she was unaware of the moan forming as he shifted for their swift merging.

"I'm sorry about that collapse last night," Yale apologized while sipping his coffee after their hurried dressing.

She buttered a toasted muffin to share with him, wishing she could have prepared a more substantial breakfast and had time to enjoy it more leisurely. But he had given her the options . . .

"You needed your sleep," she interrupted. How she wished she felt free to tell him to bring clothes so he could save time by not having to go home to change on the mornings he slept over. But for some reason she couldn't shake the feeling she was walking a fine line with him and had to let him set the pace. She didn't even dare offer him a key again.

"Things should be less hectic today," he said as they kissed good-bye. "Do you think I dare suggest we try for that dinner I still owe you?"

She met the twinkle in his eye with a teasing smile. "I'll have a nice steak ready just in case we don't make it!"

"Promises, promises," he said goadingly as they descended in the elevator. They parted at their cars, Hannah glowing from the deep contentment mushrooming in her. How she loved that man!

They didn't make the dinner that night, and Yale departed after they sat down to the steak at ten o'clock. Hannah spent a thoughtful hour after he left cleaning the kitchen and, when finished, wandering around the living room, fluffing pillows and straightening with restless fingers.

She knew what her problem was—had been unsuccessfully trying to bury it. Their lovemaking was more than wonderful, but she couldn't still the nagging intrusion that no matter how completely she gave of herself, Yale was still holding back an infinitesimal but vital part of himself. Why she had that feeling, she didn't know, or why it should be important to her. By now she couldn't even be certain that there had been a difference in the beginning and tried to rationalize that it was all part of her imagination. But still . . .

Yale had warned her that he'd be too busy the next two days to see her. "The heavy presses will be in and, when going over the floor plans with Winthrop, we saw some needed changes, so we have to be there to see that they're placed correctly before they get bolted to the floor. That means some of the electric cables will have to be realigned, among other things."

She assured him of her understanding. Besides, the quicker this all was done, she rationalized, the sooner they could reach some degree of normalcy.

The next two days passed without his coming, though he called to explain that while everything was running smoothly, it was taking longer than anticipated. She was sound asleep when the phone rang Saturday night and she peered bleary-eyed at the clock to groan on seeing it was after midnight. She picked up the receiver and smiled sleepily on hearing the deep purr.

"If you're dreaming, it better be about me," Yale said softly.

"I am and it is, and if you'll hang up I can get back to it before I miss the good part," she teased.

"Wretch!" he laughed. "I just got back from the plant and have decided enough is enough. Tomorrow is Sunday and I'm declaring a holiday, and as a prize for your long-suffering patience I plan to take you for a picnic on the boat."

"Mmm, nice. And for that auspicious occasion, I'll wear my new bikini, or whatever one calls the scraps of lace I paid an exorbitant price for."

There was a moment's silence before he groaned. "You're not playing fair. My imagination is playing all sorts of tricks on me and here I am, facing an empty bed."

"Complaints, complaints!" she answered throatily. "What time does this holiday begin?"

"Eleven o'clock?" he suggested. "By then I should have had enough sack time under my belt and feel more normal."

"Shall I pack the picnic?"

A huge yawn came over the phone telling of his exhaustion. "I was hoping you'd offer. I'll bring the champagne."

"Are we celebrating something special?" she asked with interest.

"Two things. The worst of the pressure is over at the plant, and I'll have the day with my girl. Sleep tight, sweet heart."

"Sleep tight, my love," she whispered.

The day was perfect for sailing. The sky was a clear cerulean blue with little puffs of cloud, and Hannah hoped fervently they wouldn't grow into the angry thunderheads later in the afternoon as they frequently did during the summer in Florida.

Yale greeted her with nuzzling kisses, then moved her

abruptly away from him. "We both know where that will lead to if we don't get out of here," he said firmly.

"And you're hungry as usual," she teased, not hiding how breathless his kisses had made her.

"Always," he confirmed, his eyes smoking over her. He scooped up the picnic hamper waiting by the door while she slung her canvas carryall over her shoulder and hurried to follow him. She was wearing old jeans torn off mid-calf and a bright yellow shirt tied at her waist. The promised bikini was underneath and, while dressing, visions had risen in anticipation of his expression when she disrobed before him after the sails were set and he was relaxed at the tiller.

He was wearing a thin knit shirt and faded denims that permitted her to drink in the play of muscles along his shoulders and the way his biceps bulged as he lifted the containers into the trunk. Whom was she fooling? she asked herself when sliding into the seat. She was the one anticipating seeing him in his brief bathing suit, her pulse already leaping with the knowledge of how his magnificent torso always affected her.

The ocean was fairly calm and they sailed out the Palm Beach Inlet to enjoy an hour's run on the sparkling water before returning to drop the anchor where they had before. The remaining lines of weariness on Yale's face had disappeared under the therapeutic effect from the clean salty breeze and the lilting lap of the water against the hull.

His reaction had been all she'd expected when she'd balanced in the cockpit and had removed her outer garments. "Whatever you paid for that, it was worth it," he growled from deep in his throat and she knew he saw how her nipples hardened under the anticipation behind his words.

This time he'd made certain that the hatches had been

opened so the cooler ocean breezes had aired out the cabin. After the anchor had been dropped they took a refreshing swim, then, letting his eyes do their urging, he took her hand and drew her below.

He held her for long seconds, as if savoring the softness of her body melded against his. "Do you think I'll ever have enough of you in my arms?" he said at last.

Please, never! she wanted to cry, but she smiled dreamily while her fingertips moved caressingly over the outline of his face. How she loved him! she agonized, then, acting on instinct, she pushed him onto the bunk so she was looking down at him. Always before he had controlled the lovemaking and her response had been uninhibited, but now, for some reason, she felt the need to be the initiator. She bent down and took his mouth with slow deliberation. It was her lips that urged his to part, so she could sup the inner honey in the moist recesses. He seemed to sense her need to do her own exploring and stretched out on the bunk, his fingertips running up and down her spine his only contribution to her act.

The gentle rise and fall of the boat created its own pulse beat, and the small cabin became a perfect and snug harbor waiting for the expression of her love.

She left his mouth with a reluctant sigh and began searching out the warm areas he had taught her about. Her tongue flicked over his earlobe before she ground it gently with her teeth, the slightly salty taste a stimulating accent. The warmth of his neck took her interest next and her lips rested on the pulse moving heavily in its curve.

Her hands tested the path before her mouth followed, leaving a trail of kisses so she could find her way back. Her fingers led her tongue in teasing the hard pebble of his nipples. She tugged and soothed the hair covering his chest, loving the silky-rough spring of it even while vibrantly conscious of the increased thunder of his heartbeat so close to her ear.

She moved lower, her hands following the hair-covered path, pulling, kneading over his flat abdomen, thrillingly aware of how each exploratory sweep caused his muscles to quiver and tense under her manipulation. When she reached his bathing trunks, he raised his hips to facilitate their removal. She was made immediately aware of the effect of her lovemaking and she quivered in response, allowing she was a victim of her own seduction.

Her leg slid over his, and only then did she realize Yale had already untied the strings of her bikini and she was as naked as he. She raised her hips to settle over him, a sensuous sigh escaping at the exquisite sensations running through her as the tender skin of her inner thigh reacted to the stimulus of his hair-rough legs. He clasped her hips firmly and the reins were given over to him as he guided her into the thrills of this new position.

The sharp rocking of the boat woke them from their short nap. Her head turned on the pillow and her heart swelled with a new emotion on seeing his smile of pure contentment, knowing she had put it there. "Time to feed me, woman," he said.

"I seem to recall hearing that before," she pouted. "Don't you think it's time to reverse that role?"

She gave a protesting squeal when he rose threateningly over her and she backtracked quickly. "Perhaps if you ask prettily," she inserted, batting her lashes coquettishly.

"I'm afraid to," he growled with meaning. "You keep taking advantage of me."

She burst into laughter at the thought of him ever losing control of any situation. Even with her lovemaking, she had only been duplicating his teachings.

He reached for his trunks and they then spent hilarious

minutes searching for her wisps of lace before finding them wedged between the bunk and the hull.

A new peace filled Hannah. She couldn't place her finger on why, but by the time they upped anchor and sailed back to the marina, their relationship seemed to have somehow settled onto a new plane. And when they'd stowed their gear in the trunk of the car and Yale cupped her face for a kiss, she sensed he felt it too. What it presaged she didn't know, but she glowed with an inner satisfaction she never knew before and prayed that it meant he was recognizing a deepening commitment. When they passed several small children playing along the park fronting the waterway, an overwhelming yearning rose to hold a dark-haired, gray-eyed boy in her arms . . . Yale's son . . . and the thought made her catch her breath.

They sped across the Flagler Bridge leading to Palm Beach and she arched a brow at him in question when he headed north to his house instead of to her apartment.

"I'll take a quick shower and change before taking you home," he informed her. "It's become a challenge and this time I intend that nothing will stop me from that dinner date I've been promising you."

She chuckled with delight over the whys and wherefores that caused the dinner never to materialize. "Don't you think you're tempting fate by announcing it out loud?" she teased. "Perhaps we should just sneak up on it." Already she was wondering if the servants were there or if this was their Sunday off. But then there was Lois and her son, Jay, she remembered and gave up her half-formed notion.

A frown creased his brow when they turned into his drive. A dark blue car sat there, a sticker on it proclaiming it a rental. His frown deepened when after escorting Hannah up the steps, he found the door unlocked. "Wait here," he ordered tersely as he moved cautiously through the door.

Her heart thudded heavily in her chest, but she followed him instinctively, unable to have him facing an unknown assailant without her by his side. The large entrance foyer was empty, but the sound of an angry voice could be heard coming from the living room. Yale strode over swiftly with Hannah at his heels. The frown had become a thunderhead, alerting her that he recognized the voices and that anger had replaced the concern.

They halted at the doorway to take in the tableau. Lois stood in the middle of the room, her head thrown back in defiance, a protective hand on her son's shoulder as he clung to her skirt. His eyes were wide with uncomprehending bewilderment. Both faces appeared ashen as they stared at the threatening blond-haired man before them.

"I didn't have to look far for you, did I?" the man grated out. "Where else would you run to but back into your lover's arms?"

"I refuse to listen to your jealous mouthings any longer, Jace," Lois returned in a fierce hiss. "I'm tired of trying to make you understand that Yale is my cousin, even the brother I never had, and nothing more."

"And I'm tired of hearing how wonderful he is, how successful his business is, how perfect his home is, and all the money he's dripping with!" he snarled. "What's the matter, isn't a cleaning woman once a week enough for you? I'm sorry if you decided you want to live like a queen, but you're still my wife and you're coming back with me even if I have to drag you all the way."

He lurched forward and for the first time Hannah realized he must have been drinking. Yale moved in long swift strides to stand protectively before Lois.

"Hello, Jace," he said calmingly. "I didn't know you

were coming. If you had called, we'd have met you at the airport."

The man reared up and Hannah saw that, while he was inches shorter than Yale, he was still strongly built. "Ah, lover boy to the rescue," he cried derisively. "You'd better step aside if you don't want your pretty face messed up. I'm not going to let you have what belongs to me no matter what you lure her away with!"

"Lois belongs to no one. She's her own person," Yale said, his measured words giving a hint to the temper being held under tight control. "And once you clear yourself of your unreasonable jealousy she might find it possible to live with you again."

Jay took that moment to leave his mother's side and attach himself to Yale's leg. From that greater protection he peered at his father, his face puckered in confusion.

On seeing the two sets of identical gray eyes and matching black hair, the man let out a roar of anguished rage. "Do you deny him?" he shouted. "Is this the son I've been praying for, the bastard hiding under my name?"

Horror crashed through Hannah on hearing the declaration that was so close to her first reaction. But she'd traveled far since then. She was still warm from Yale's lovemaking, but beyond her love, every reasoning part of her knew that he could never have done what was being insinuated. While a very virile man, his character would never permit him to consider a liaison, however fleeting, with a cousin he loved as a sister.

The air was electric under the ugly accusation. A white line traced Yale's mouth and a rational man would have quailed on seeing the fury raging in his eyes, but Jace's florid face showed he was fast stepping beyond all control.

"You're being quite obtuse, Mr. Dorminor," Hannah said coolly into the heated air. She was astounded on hearing her voice, but something drove her to do something to defuse the dangerous situation.

The man turned with a start, for the first time realizing there was someone else in the room. "Surely you've heard of the laws of heredity," she continued sharply. How dare he use those vile terms about Yale! "Can you give me one reason besides your jealousy why Lois shouldn't be carrying some of the same genes and chromosomes as her cousin, and why gray eyes shouldn't be one of the traits that she's able to pass on to her children?"

She saw that while he was handsome enough, his rage and drink had distorted his face into an unpleasant mask. Had he been fortifying himself with drinks on the long trip from the West Coast, where they lived?

"Who the devil are you?" he asked rudely.

"I'm a friend of Yale's," she returned with ill-concealed dislike. "He's explained to me his love for Lois and it's nothing like what you have dreamed up." Her gaze reached across the man's shoulder and locked on Yale's eyes as she continued. "If my sister ever found herself in the same predicament as Lois, I would open my home to her in the same way. It's as simple as that. You should be ashamed to deny the wonderful son you have." She paused, conscious of something new in the swirling smoke of Yale's eyes, something that warmed even as it burned.

"Daddy, daddy . . . up!" The chubby boy had enough of the uncomfortable atmosphere around him and reached up his arms to be lifted in the strong ones that represented security.

Jace stiffened before gazing down and saw the confusion wrinkling the small face. A groan erupted from deep within him as he fell to his knees to gather the boy close.

"I wanna go home," Jay lisped. A chubby hand moved over the beard-rough cheek and Jace's face held such stark pain that Hannah's throat closed in a spasm of pity. She had experienced the corroding result of jealousy and could imagine how his doubts must have been torturing him.

Hannah's attention shifted to Lois to find that her anger was gone, to be replaced by a look of shocked awareness. Could it be that she hadn't known the extent of her husband's love and what her actions had provoked? She watched as Lois took a hesitant step, then another, before running across the room to drop down beside Jace rocking his son in his arms.

"Oh, darling, I didn't realize!" she sobbed, her hands raised imploringly as tears streamed down her cheeks.

Jace freed an arm to include her in his embrace. "Don't cry, love. Please, stop. I'm not worth it." His lips touched her lids with tender kisses until he realized the tableau they presented.

"Come, let's get out of here," he muttered gruffly, embarrassed over the public display. He staggered slightly when rising, but his grasp was firm on his wife and son's hands when he paused before Yale. "I'm sorry, old man," he apologized.

Yale nodded briefly in answer and watched his departure with an evaluating eye before following them out of the room.

Hannah found herself too abashed by her precipitant behavior to move. Yet she was aware of the remnants of the fierce need to protect what had invaded her and had caused her to intrude in what was a family problem. Still, how dare the man attack Yale's character! part of her steamed while her cooler head wondered over what Yale was thinking about her brash words.

Vaguely she heard the front door open and what sounded like agitated voices before the door closed again. Was the fool Jace still putting up an argument?

The footfalls on the marble floor warned of Yale's return and she looked at him in trepidation. He stood, hands on hips, and stared at her with an unreadable expression.

"I'm glad you're playing on my side, tiger," he said softly, the lines spidering the corners of his eyes deepening in silent laughter. "I didn't know you possessed such a protective streak in you!"

What could she say—that she'd defy the devil himself if he tried to harm him? She was too overwhelmed herself to fully understand the strong emotion that had assailed her.

She gave a weak smile, then sobered on contemplating the self-inflicted torture under which Jace had been suffering. Hadn't she been a victim also, though thankfully to a lesser degree? "I can feel sorry for the misguided fool," she murmured. "Do you think you'll ever be able to hammer some sense into him?"

"It seems Lois is starting on the project," he said with a grin. Seeing her start of surprise, he explained further. "Lois thankfully wasn't letting him drive in his condition. He wasn't having any of it, but she talked him down quickly, telling him she wasn't going to feel guilty about the death of her son's father if he killed himself while driving in his condition. I believe his accusations today hit her hard. I don't think she had any idea that by phoning me so often she was feeding his jealousy. It's another case of two people hurting each other by not talking things out."

His meaning was clear and she dropped her head in contrition. They'd suffered through their own trauma because of her.

His finger moved under her chin, lifting her face for his inspection. There was something new in his eyes, a brilliance she'd caught only a glimpse of when she had come to his defense after Jace's crude accusation.

"You meant it, didn't you, about having no doubts

about Jay's parentage." His voice held the deep purr that, as usual, turned her legs into unsupporting rubber. His finger moved to trace the lower curve of her lip. "You've finally learned to trust me."

Her nod brought her mouth against his finger and she placed a kiss on it. The action sparked additional lights in his eyes. "I always will," she promised in a whisper, but she didn't know if he heard her; his mouth was already claiming hers. She sensed the difference at once. Behind the firm possession there was a dedication, and her whole body surged in ecstacy in response to the silent avowal of love.

When he drew his mouth from hers in a reluctant admission of the need for air, he cushioned her head on his shoulder while cradling her loosely in the circle of his arms. She was vibrantly aware that steel lay under the wrapping of tenderness with which he held her, warning her that while she had freedom of movement, he would never let her far from the boundary of his arms. She nestled closer, letting him know she freely accepted the limitation.

"Come upstairs with me, Hannah. There's something I want to show you . . ."

"Is this a new theme on 'come up and see my etchings'?" she asked archly over her breathlessness. How easily he could do that to her!

"No," he said solemnly. "I want you to see the bedroom you're going to share with me from now on. While your bed is fine, I'm tired of traipsing between the two. Besides, I'll never tolerate a wife sleeping anyplace but in my room!"

She stopped in her tracks. "Yale," she said in a quiet voice that told of her seriousness. "Don't tease me about something like this. Don't ever use that word unless you mean it."

His hands cupped her face in gentle possession. "Sweet heart, don't you know that from the first time I had you in bed and felt the fire you so beautifully shared with me that I already claimed you as my wife? But I needed your final commitment of trust before I could put the ring on your finger. I needed it so desperately, and knew you had it in you to give, but I couldn't demand it; it had to come freely from you."

His mouth took hers in a tender sharing that brought tears to her eyes. It wasn't until much later that she smiled with drowsy resignation as she snuggled closer to his warm body. They had done it again and had forgotten their dinner reservation.